THE REDHEAD IN THE COVE

THE REDHEAD IN THE COVE

SCOTT ADDEO YOUNG AND EDMOND G. ADDEO

Congrats, ~~Sandy~~ !

Ed Addeo

Thank you so much ~~Sandy~~ !
Appreciate the effort 7·20·2021

Waterside Productions

Cover artwork and design by David Danz, Placerville, Calif.

Printed in the United States of America

First Printing, 2021

ISBN-13: 978-1-951805-39-5 print edition
ISBN-13: 978-1-951805-40-1 ebook edition

Waterside Productions
2055 Oxford Ave
Cardiff, CA 92007
www.waterside.com

To our family, in gratitude for their Gibraltar-like patience.

SAY
EGA

TABLE OF CONTENTS

ACKNOWLEDGEMENTS

If I've met you, thank you.
If I haven't, I hope to.

The authors would like to acknowledge the indispensible help of San Francisco Police Officer Dustin Daza (also Captain, US Army Reserve); Drs. Scott Sinnott, M.D., Irina DeFisher, M.D. and Michael Charles, M.D.; internationally-known forensic scientist John DeHaan, Ph.D.; Richard Spotswood, LL.B.; editor par excellence Jerry Bires; our many patient beta readers; and, of course, the encouragement and support of friends and relatives up and down the state of California.

SAY, Santa Barbara, CA
EGA, Mill Valley, CA

CHAPTER ONE

In his gleaming yellow kayak, Freddy Davis had been floating in McCovey Cove behind Oracle Park all afternoon waiting for a souvenir home run baseball to splash near enough for him to grab. But even though Freddy wouldn't snatch a ball from the chilly San Francisco Bay water today, it was still about to become a day he would remember for the rest of his life.

He had been patrolling in his kayak around the cove for the past hour, listening to the radio stream of the Giants game through the earbuds on his iPhone. The bay was unusually calm, the customary morning fog had lifted, and now only occasional wisps of clouds quickly dissipated over the East Bay hills. There wasn't a whitecap in sight as Freddy paddled thankfully in slow circles in his new vessel, waiting patiently for the exciting moment to happen. It was a Malibu Two XL tandem kayak, designed especially for rough water, although those features weren't needed today. It came standard with two seats and bungee lashings over the front and rear tank wells, but he had converted it to a one-paddler by removing the bow seat and re-positioning the other to the center. He did a lot of kayaking and this was perfect for the generally choppy currents.

Freddy was in an inlet of the China Basin section of the bay just behind the right field wall of arguably the most beautiful baseball stadium in the Major Leagues. The database vendor Oracle had paid three hundred million dollars for the naming rights, so the park was now called Oracle Park. But to Oracle founder Larry Ellison's chagrin, the fondly remembered ballpark was still referred to by stubborn fans—who tenaciously clung to the glorious half-decade when the Giants had won three World Series in five seasons—as Pac Bell Park. One of the most prominent features of the ballpark, beside the gigantic Coke bottle and the enormous three-fingered fielder's mitt above the left field stands—an exact replica of the team owner's childhood glove—is the red brick right field wall, which is precisely twenty-four feet high in honor of the great Giants Hall-of-Famer Willie Mays, who wore number 24 his entire career. And ever since San Francisco Giants fans realized that a baseball floats in salt water, it became a favorite enterprise of all kinds of boat enthusiasts, from rowboats and paddleboards to million-dollar yachts, to hang out in McCovey Cove behind that wall on game day and wait for a home run to clear the wall and splash into the bay.

The cove, named after the feared left-handed Giants first baseman Willie McCovey, who hit 519 career homers over several dozen miscellaneous right field walls, is actually the entrance to an estuary that runs under the Lefty O'Doul Bridge—sometimes called the 3rd Street Bridge by the unwashed—and out into Mission Bay to the south. It is bounded right outside the right field wall by a long pier onto which boats and ferries can load and unload fans from surrounding counties directly to the stadium, and across the inlet by a small park with a statue of McCovey, and a shoreline protected by riprap—small granite boulders the size of Volkswagen engines that protect the shoreline from erosion and, unofficially, from unattended children and animals.

Freddy was a muscular first baseman on the Sacred Heart High School baseball varsity team, now enjoying the last week of summer vacation. He'd done this floating patrol seven times so far this season, and eight times last season, but due to bad luck, banjo hitters, and pitching duels—not to mention speedier boats surrounding him—he had yet to retrieve a home run from the cove. One of his classmates had fished one out last year and had brought it into class to show his jealous friends. Freddy was determined to get one this summer, but so far... zip, zero, zilch. It even made him long for the return of baseball's infamous steroid era when jacked-up hitters such as Bonds, McGuire, and Sosa homered with juice-induced regularity.

He floated next to a 60-foot sailboat filled with laughing bikini-clad beauties and their boyfriends barbequing on the stern and watching a large TV with drinks in their hands. Freddy enjoyed surreptitiously ogling the girls as he circled their boat, even imagining that a few of them were close to his age. One of the girls threw him an olive, and when he graciously threw it back, they enjoyed a brief game of catch until he drifted out of range.

Even though he couldn't make out the images on the boat's TV screen, the audio was loud enough across the water that he could undo his earbuds and clearly hear Jon Miller's calling of the game. Between Miller's excitability and the explosive roar of the crowd, the cove floaters could tell when a possible home run was coming their way.

Such as now, with both the crowd suddenly erupting in a roar and Miller shouting, "He hits it a long way to right, long and high ..."

The floaters' eyes all turned in unison to the top of the right field wall, searching for the prized tiny white dot. Freddy picked it up as it sailed over the wall on the other side of the yellow foul pole. It wouldn't count on the scoreboard, but in the water, a foul ball was just as prized as a fair one.

Now he strenuously paddled his kayak toward the ball as it splashed, and he sped with the incoming tide toward the Lefty O'Doul Bridge. But just then a motorized Boston Whaler whizzed past him in a flash of bubbly wake, its owner beating him to the ball, scooping it up in a fishing net, and roaring away, triumphantly waving the soaking souvenir in a raised fist as he went.

A dejected Freddy nevertheless realized he was going full speed toward the bridge and swerved sharply left, heading toward the rip-rap stones at the shore of McCovey Park on the far side.

That was when he saw the strange-looking red seaweed. It was draped over one of the small granite boulders at the waterline, and he thought it peculiar enough to take a closer look.

When he got there, he was stunned.

Even sickened.

It wasn't red seaweed.

It was the long red hair of a naked dead woman wedged face down amid the rocks.

CHAPTER TWO

Steve Lombardi stood and clapped his hands vigorously as his favorite piano player, Larry Dahl, finished a fabulous "Swanee River Boogie," his fingers just a flashing blur across the keys. A fan of classic jazz violinists and guitarists, one of Steve's favorite musical pieces was "Hora Staccato," a supremely difficult classical composition by Jascha Heifitz, the celebrated violinist, but Steve had never heard it played on the piano. The generally accepted story goes that it was originally composed by a Romanian concert musician named Grigoras Dinicu, and that Heifitz simply arranged it into its currently played, and most popular, version.

The piece was full of sixteenth- and thirty-second notes requiring exceptional fingering, and was rarely heard being played by anyone, much less a saloon piano player. When Steve had first encountered Dahl at Marin Joe's, a restaurant/bar in Marin County, and asked him if he could play it, Dahl smiled knowingly, thinking it an especially diabolical request, perhaps some kind of a trick. Dahl thought a moment, eyeing this stranger.

"You ever heard it on the piano?" he asked, hands still in his lap. "It was written as a violin piece."

"I know, but I heard it once on the marimba," Steve said. "And on a cruise once some guy from Peru or somewhere tried it on the flute. And then some guy really messed it up on an accordion in some beer joint in Coney Island."

"But not piano?"

"Nah," Steve said, smiling. "But after that boogie, I'd bet you can."

"Well, it's been a while, but I'll give it a try."

Dahl then launched into an impossibly perfect rendition on his keyboard. Steve was absolutely stunned, and became an avid Dahl groupie, following him at various local venues around the Bay Area and considering him the best piano player west of the Mississippi.

Now Dahl was finishing up a Friday night gig at Pier 23, a small-ish seafood bistro on San Francisco's Embarcadero that featured jazz music every night of the week and Sunday afternoons. It was a time-honored San Francisco establishment located right on the bay. It featured a wide deck for waterside dining on mild days and a cozy interior on the usually chilly and foggy nights. It was family owned and operated, and featured Maryland-style crab cakes, fish & chips, and raw oysters. Local musicians liked it because of its cozy atmosphere in the evenings and its high-tipping customers.

Dahl stood, downed the last of his brandy—Armagnac, a distinctive kind of brandy produced in the Armagnac region in Gascony, southwest France, the only brandy he drank—and started collecting his music sheets. He was a short man, sixtyish, with long, curly auburn hair beginning to go grey, the remnants of teenage acne still evident on his cheeks, and wore a seemingly perpetual grin. He hailed from Cleveland, where his father was first chair violin in the Cleveland Orchestra under George Szell. He'd spent most of his career either performing in various jazz groups in and around New Orleans, or "on the ships," meaning behemoth-sized cruise ships circling the globe. During one fateful cruise, he jumped ship in San Francisco and spent his time since then earning a living teaching and playing in local hotels and restaurants.

Before he could reach for his tip jar to empty its contents, Steve also got up, quickly balled up a fiver and deftly lofted it into the jar just before Dahl could overturn it.

"Three pointer! Nice shot, Steve. And thanks again," Dahl said.

"You never disappoint, Larry."

"You're certainly my best fan in the Bay Area," Dahl said. "I really appreciate it."

"At least your oldest, maybe."

Dahl waved to the room. "Nah, you see lots of gray heads, don't you?"

Steve laughed. "Our kind of music," he said. "Where do you go next?"

"The Mystic in Petaluma tomorrow and Sunday, then 19 Broadway in Fairfax next weekend. After that, weekends at Marin Joe's again."

"Catch you in Fairfax," Steve said, shaking hands. "If not, Marin Joe's for sure." He gulped the rest of his scotch and headed for the men's room at the end of the bar.

Outside, the moon was high and full, but only a dim disc in the filtering fog as Steve tugged at his Aran Island turtleneck and decided to walk to the Ferry Building for a nightcap. The foghorn atop the Golden Gate Bridge bellowed its intermittent warning, a lonely, peculiarly romantic moan. He was playing a Dahl tune in his mind as he strolled, a version of the Beatles' "Something," when he heard what sounded like a woman's shriek. He stopped abruptly, listening. It was either that or a seagull's squawk, which always sounded to him like the sound of desperation. At first, he couldn't tell from which direction it came. He had just passed a run-down dive called Shaky's, mostly inhabited by drunks and out-of-work longshoremen, and he was now alongside a deserted wharf. He peered into the dark shadows of the wharf but saw nothing. He decided to backtrack and at the end of a long parking lot he spotted a dark three-story office building on the other side of the wharf, its only light coming from a single second-story window. He listened intently.

Nothing again.

Retracing a few more steps he looked back at the entrance to Shaky's but didn't see anything unusual. He stepped to the door and eased it open, seeing only an assortment of mostly disheveled late-nighters at the bar or inebriated patrons trying to dance to annoyingly dissonant sounds coming from a dimly lit jukebox. He let the door slam shut and shook his head at the difference between this off-key mess and his friend Larry Dahl's melodious keyboard.

Steve walked on.

He took a few more steps onto the wharf and was about to decide what he'd heard was just a seagull squawking when, next to a dim 40-watt bare bulb attached to a metal sheet that indicated it was the back door of Shaky's bar, he thought he saw several figures moving along a low wall. Then he heard a frightened *yelp* again; definitely female.

He turned and walked slowly toward the figures and made out that there were three men grappling with a young woman. As he got closer, he saw that one of them wore the uniform of a sailor, and by the polished shoes of the other two in civvies he surmised that they too were off-duty swabbies. The woman looked only about twenty-five or so, and wore a bolero jacket over a turtleneck and denim skirt. One of the guys in civvies was holding the girl's arms behind her while the sailor groped drunkenly at her chest and the other civvies guy was making a kissy face at her.

"Hey!" Steve yelled. "Knock it off!"

The trio turned in unison as the girl freed herself and backed against the wall. Surprised, the sailor pointed back to the street. "Mind your own business, gramps. Beat it!"

Steve looked them over carefully, eyes adapting to the light from the dim bulb. They'd obviously been drinking, most likely in the dive he just passed. The sailor's uniform was rumpled, and Steve momentarily wondered where his cap was. One of them had a bright blond crew cut, almost white, and swayed as he sized up Steve. The third was massive, with wide shoulders and about six-five, Steve guessed. He had been holding the girl and now stood with his hands on his hips, a satisfied smirk on his face.

Blondie gestured toward the large one. "Get him outta here, Benny."

"You don't want no trouble, guy," Benny said as he stepped toward Steve. Blondie and Sailor also started closing in. The girl stiffly hugged the wall.

"And neither does she, if I'm not mistaken," Steve said. "Maybe she'd rather go home with me."

Sailor laughed. "Better fuck off," he said. "You might get hurt."

Steve just smiled at him. "I seriously doubt it," he said.

"You doubt what?" Pointing an index finger at Steve's chest.

"I doubt I'm going to get hurt." He looked toward the girl. "You OK, miss?"

She whimpered, nodding a *yes*. Steve now guessed she was no older than twenty, twenty-one.

As Steve looked at her, Benny suddenly lunged at him. Steve jabbed out his open right palm in a lightning nanosecond, crushing Benny's nose up into his skull, while simultaneously slashing the edge of his left hand into the throat of oncoming Blondie. As Benny dropped like an abandoned ventriloquist's dummy and Blondie grasped his neck, gutturally choking and gasping for breath, Steve turned to Sailor who was now charging him in a karate-like attack. Sailor started a chop but Steve deftly sidestepped and grabbed his wrist in a vice-like grip and twisted until he felt the grinding of gristle and bone as Sailor's elbow and shoulder snapped like a dried turkey wishbone. His scream echoed off the wharf walls, drowning out the girl's new scream.

It was over in eight seconds.

With the crumpled and motionless Benny on the ground, Blondie on his knees still choking helplessly, and Sailor twirling and hopping like a crippled ballerina, grabbing his shoulder and continuing his agonizing screams, Steve turned to the girl.

"You OK?"

She was straightening her jacket and skirt and staring wide-eyed at Steve. "My God," she said. "Where did *you* come from?"

"You know these guys?" Steve jerked his thumb toward the dive. "You been in that joint?"

She shook her head and jerked her own thumb at the office building on the other side of the wharf. "Working late at the Harbor Services Union, because I'm going on vacation next week. I was walking to my car when they came out of the bar." She pointed to a lone yellow Toyota at the far edge of the wharf.

"Really bad idea parking so far away. C'mon, I'll walk you." He took her arm and they started toward the car.

"There were lots of cars around when I got here this morning," she said. "The whole lot was jammed and it was the only open spot." Then she stopped and looked at him again. "That was pretty impressive, mister. How old *are* you?"

"How about them Giants?" Steve said.

CHAPTER THREE

Look, I'm sixty-five years old, OK? But I'm in better shape than anyone I know. Except, maybe, for some young cops I still drink with now and then. So yes, I take Flomax and I put Les Paul and Mary Ford on my iTunes, and some Mantovani, and Charlie Chaplin's "Terry's Theme" from the movie *Limelight*, although I've recently moved forward a few decades and discovered Mark Knopfler's Dire Straits and Chris Isaak. I'm still a few decades behind the artists of this century. Besides, none of them can match Stephane Grappelli or Django Reinhardt.

So, call me retro-Gramps.

I manage to work out every other day, use the free weights and most of the machines at the Mill Valley Rec Center, plus I alternate jogging each day at three miles on even-numbered days and ten miles on the odd numbers. To keep myself distracted I usually jog around the Bayfront Park, watching practically every known breed of dog frolicking in the special doggie area, as well, I must admit, the daily contingent of female dog walkers. Or else I head along the bike path leading south to Sausalito and the Golden Gate Bridge, and featuring a fabulous view of Mount Tamalpais on the way back. Lately I've been stopping briefly to watch a small group of guys older than me fooling with their respective airplane drones. Turns out they're all ex-military pilots, mostly F-86 Sabre Jet guys from the Korean War, probably in their late eighties by now, and a few F-105 Starfighter Navy guys from Vietnam. It's fun watching them do all sorts of aerobatics with the drones, and even dogfighting each other for who buys the beer at lunchtime.

And just a month ago, behind a bar on the Embarcadero, I beat the crap out of three guys molesting a young girl. I seem to have this soft spot for women getting slapped around by drunken men. Saw enough of that when I was in the service myself— and after that scene at Shaky's, it does not seem like enough has changed.

I'm not bragging—it's just that I'm starting to feel my age and I have to admit I don't like it. I haven't checked, but if you go to the Sacramento Hall of Meaningless Records you might find out I'm really not the oldest practicing P.I. in the state. But it sure feels like it sometimes. I doubt the rest of the world has such a job description.

Me personally? Pretty average, really. I grew up on 24th Street in San Francisco's Mission District, had a 3.8 GPA at Saint Ignatius High, which got me into Notre Dame, where I played second-string football and learned to pluck the banjo in the school band. I graduated with a B.A. in Psychology, but it didn't take me long to discover that such a degree qualifies one for absolutely nothing without a following M.A. So instead of wasting time looking for a non-existent job, I decided to join the service and spend a few years thinking about the future.

I decided on the Navy, for several reasons. First, their recruiting slogan at the time, "Join the Navy and See the World," had definitely worked on me. Second, after checking with several co-ed friends, I decided that naval officers' uniforms were the handsomest of all. Especially if you wore a pilot's gold wings or a submariner's golden twin porpoises, but which a failed eye test in the N.R.O.T.C. exam rendered impossible for me. And third, I always heard that the food in the Navy, especially in submarines, was the best of all the services.

So I became a Naval Officer, in a neat-looking uniform, but didn't get to wear it much in a still-undisclosed top-secret military engagement in Panama. But that's also one of the things I try not to think about.

When I got out I spent some time as Chief of Security at one of the largest Silicon Valley semiconductor companies, got tired of corporate work and busked around for a year playing the banjo in a mostly rum-sodden group called "The Black Bananas" in a Palo Alto college pub on Emerson Street, hard by Stanford University, then did a fifteen-year stint with the San Francisco Police Department as a Homicide Investigator; spent a year bumming around the world after that, and finally decided to settle down and go out and start my own private investigator business.

At first it looked like a bad decision. It was tough. I was too used to succeeding to run up against failure. I mean, I didn't argue when my prematurely white hair mistakenly got me senior discounts at the movies; and ten percent off motel rates was fine; even a few bucks less on the golf cart fee when they asked "walking or riding?" was fine. What was *not* fine was when potential clients saw my white hair and suddenly announced they still had other investigators to interview.

Thank God for Johnny Lynch. He was my SFPD Inspector partner with whom I worked closely on several homicide cases over the years. We became close friends. (Incidentally, SFPD detectives aren't called detectives. They're called Inspectors. At least they used to be until they did away with that title about ten years ago. Don't ask me why they were called that. Seems to me you can either detect or inspect, one or the other. In New York they detect. In San Francisco they inspect. I suppose the good ones *could* detect and then inspect. Or even do both simultaneously.)

But where was I?

He was a handsome devil—still is—and twenty years younger than me. I frequently used him as a chick magnet in various San Francisco saloons.

Johnny had thrown a few small cases my way—no biggies but enough to buy the Cheerios. He was a shameless softie, always secretly dropping twenty-dollar bills into the open handbags or pockets of down-trodden men and women on the streets, or over-tipping the waiters at Hunters Point, tired from serving drunken patrons returning from 49er games at the now-demolished Candlestick Park.

Anyway, Johnny called me late one afternoon at my place in the Marin County hills. Business had been slow, which is to say normal, and I was spending some time attending to little housekeeping details I'd been putting off. My little condo was on the foggier side of the little cul-de-sac town of Mill Valley, and could get a bit chilly. I bought the place years ago when it was still affordable for younger working stiffs. A fellow cop was retiring and moving to Portland to be close to his grandkids and made me a deal I couldn't pass up. Now, I put some new insulation around the front door and a few windows. I also re-painted every room, un-stuck a kitchen cabinet, put in new marble countertops, re-potted a lot of sickly orchid plants, and did a quick but overdue re-finishing and vacuum job on the floors. Today, I thought about practicing on my old banjo, which was collecting dust in a corner with my softball bat and mitt, but instead I went through a stack of outdated magazines on my glass coffee table and threw them in my recycling box by the outgoing garbage bin. I didn't feel like cleaning up the kitchen sink and I hadn't made my bed in a week. So, I was in the process of cleaning my Remington 870 shotgun and Ruger LCR .38 pistol when Johnny Lynch called.

He asked how business was going lately and I told him it was drifting in the same direction as the Iraqi Stock Exchange.

"Can I buy a few shares?" he asked.

'I think it just started going up," I said. "Cost you a few UZIs."

He said he'd buy a hundred over a beer at Liverpool Lil's near the Presidio, and after I conned him into also paying my bridge fare, we agreed to meet after his shift at four p.m.

"What's going on? Can you give me something to think about on the way?" I asked.

"Got a floater," he said.

"Bad check?"

"Dead body."

"What's that got to do with me?"

"You're a baseball fan, right?"

"Is the Pope Catholic? Does a bear—" Johnny hated my clichés.

"So, you know where McCovey Cove is, right?"

"C'mon, Johnny. You giving me the 'Who's buried in Grant's Tomb?' routine?"

I heard a long sigh, then silence.

"Johnny? Are we playing 'Twenty Questions' here?"

"Look, Stevie. We got a young girl washed up right near the McCovey statue. We're all over it, but they haven't ID'd the victim yet."

I heard panic in his voice, but I couldn't figure out why. The guy'd been a cop for a hundred years and broken some spectacular cases. If you look up "tough" in the dictionary you'll see that it says, "See 'Lynch, John T.'"

"So? So?"

"So when they do, I'm in deep shit."

This was getting serious. Lynch was the cleanest cop in the history of western law enforcement, going all the way back to the Code of Hammurabi. Why was finding a dead body in San Francisco Bay problematical for my old buddy Johnny Lynch?

I said, "John, listen to me. I'm about to leave beautiful Marin County and spend twenty minutes in the fog driving to Lil's and you're hysterical about finding a body in the bay. And you're an SFPD Inspector. For chrissakes, give me something to think about on the bridge."

Silence.

"Johnny? My man?"

"Stevie," he said quietly. "When they ID her, they will think *I* might have killed her."

And he hung up.

CHAPTER FOUR

Johnny's hang-up line was like a punch in the *la bonza*—a slang Italian word for "stomach." SuperClarkKentBoyScout-cop is suspected of *killing* a girl? And she wasn't a psycho witch shoving a Glock down his throat? That couldn't have been Lynch on the phone. It had to be either a joke call or a trick of some sort. Maybe when I got to Lil's a bunch of deranged friends would jump out and yell "Happy Birthday!" Except it wasn't my birthday. And it wasn't funny. I almost knocked down the mailbox backing down my driveway.

The Golden Gate Bridge wasn't golden today. Instead, it was gripped in a thick white fog creeping across the roadway like a long roll of gauze, bouncing off Alcatraz and continuing to the East Bay as the sudden rising warmth in the Central Valley sucked the Pacific moisture eastward. Across the bridge it created a mist like cotton candy and I had to shift down and flip on my intermediate wipers. The surface was damp and traffic was slowed to a mere five m.p.h. I could barely see the tail lights of the car in front of me. Another gorgeous San Francisco late August day, when the vacationing summer tourists were caught in their Madras shorts and Hawaiian shirts freezing their buns off as they walked across the famous bridge. The *touristas* never Googled the true meaning of "summer in San Francisco."

I left the radio off and tried a few scenarios to make sense out of his comment. What could possibly be true about what he'd said? Had he accidentally knocked her off a dock somewhere? Maybe they were playing around after a drunken date and strolling the Embarcadero late at night. They had to dodge an oncoming bicyclist and in giving her a protective shove he knocked her into the water. Nah. The John I knew would have jumped in after her. Maybe he ran her over in a motorboat? Equally drunk, she insisted on water-skiing, fell in, and when he turned to get back to her, she lost her bearing and swam frantically into the props. Equally nah. John hated the water and as far as I knew never owned a boat.

It was driving me nuts. What would I come up with next? He missed a rubber band when he packed her skydiving chute? How could they think a straight-arrow cop might have killed a washed-up dead body?

I switched the radio back on and Van Morrison's "Astral Weeks" filled the silence. I wasn't sure who Van was, but I kind of liked the tune. I emerged from the strand of fog just before the toll plaza. My FasTrak transponder beeped twice as I eased through the toll booth and started to navigate the mess that was the Doyle Drive diversion reconstruction. Seems the City of San Francisco and the State of California were spending a gazillion dollars of my own tax money to protect me from some future crippling head-on collision, just because a few drunks had killed a few people over the past several decades. And in the meantime, this maze made the whole stretch of road more dangerous than before.

But where was I?

I managed to cheat death again and rolled past the old Army bungalows dotting the officers' quarters of the Presidio and the newly re-domed Palace of Fine Arts. This particular sight always settled my mind, whether coming from or going to the City. To me, it was a better city icon than the bridge or Telegraph Tower or the "pyramid" office building or any other sight. Originally built for the Pan-Pacific Exhibition in 1915, it now stood as a massive Greco-Roman domed structure with a gorgeous lagoon fronting it. It never failed to catch my eye, even now as distracted as I was.

I made a hard right on Lyon Street and eased up the hill. A few blocks later I miraculously found an early afternoon parking spot right behind Johnny's '92 black Corvette. As I crossed the street to Lil's I heard the famous Telegraph Hill parrots squawking in the eucalyptuses—eucalypti? —lining the Presidio. If you haven't heard about these screwball birds by now, Google them and read all about it. Short version: seems a few parrots escaped out a window years ago and bred a whole six or seven generations of wild parrots in the trees on and around Telegraph Hill. Must be a hundred of them by now. They lend a riot of color to the dark green background of the Presidio and nearby neighborhood of Presidio Heights and they cackle and chirp continuously. I think there's even a documentary on them somewhere on YouTube.

Liverpool Lil's is a popular funky saloon/restaurant disguised as a sports bar, a smallish narrow joint with only about fifteen tables. Four hi-def TV screens are positioned strategically around with various sports events being broadcast. The place is a shade on the dark side—no pun intended—so the TV screens always seem especially bright. Its walls are lined with old black-and-white photographs, plaques, pennants, posters, newspaper front pages, headlines, and letters, all having something to do with sports, all local high schools, colleges, and professional teams. There are lots of shots of the three Joes—DiMaggio, Louis, and Namath; plus, a subset of the three DiMaggios, Joe, Dom, and Vince, they being local boys and all. Also a few of the three Rockys—Bridges, Marciano and Balboa. Lots of heroic baseball figures from my youth, or slightly before: Ted Williams, Stan Musial, Mickey Mantle, Gil Hodges, and, of course, the "Say Hey" kid, Willie Mays. And a host of stupidly grinning politicians posing with celebrities. And starlets, lots of starlets—Marilyn, of course, being married to Joe at the time; Sophia Loren, Gina Lollobrigida and Anna Magnani, being Italian; Jane Mansfield hugging, kissing and pinching heroes of every sport, being Jane Mansfield.

The food's pretty good, too.

Johnny was sitting at a two-man alcove table by the window just inside the door and to the left of the bar. It was a tight fit, but about as private as you could get at Lil's.

I plopped down with a heave and noticed he'd already ordered my house Chardonnay. Johnny looked like hell. His straight salt-and-pepper hair was ruffled from being run through with his fingers too often and too recently. His Irish drinker's face normally would have matched his tangerine-pink golf shirt, but today his complexion was the color of a Q-Tip. It made his opal-blue eyes gleam like bright lights behind their red rims.

"So," I said. "Do I get a reward if I turn you in?"

"Do they still call you the Jerry Lewis of PIs?" he said.

"Sorry," I said. And I was. Johnny was as depressed as I'd ever seen him. "It's just that I thought you *had* to be joking."

He took a long pull on his Anchor Steam and then downed his shot of Johnny Walker Blue.

"I wish I were."

"Tell me about it. How do you know who the girl is?"

He tapped with his University of San Francisco ring on his Anchor Steam bottle and signaled for another round. I pulled on my Chardonnay. No, I don't *sip*. I pull. Like a real man. And Chardonnay is only my daytime booze; nights I'm a scotch drinker, too, except I can't afford what Johnny was drinking.

Johnny avoided my gaze and said nothing for a long while. He was either deep in thought or figuring out just how he was going to approach this conversation. Then he sighed, emptied the beer bottle, and gently, neatly, slid the bottle and the empty shot glass to the edge of the table.

"Bill Ralston, the Inspector on scene—you remember Bill?"

I thought back. "Yeah, younger guy? A trifle gung-ho, but a straight shooter and honest. He was just a new uniform when I knew him, what? Ten, twelve years ago? He's an Inspector? I thought they did away with that title."

"He learned fast. And yeah, he's the last one."

"I remember when we first met, he was just a patrolman and he kept calling me 'sir'. He can't be any more than, what? Thirty-five? Thirty-eight?"

"Around that. Came up fast. Turns out he has a degree in Criminology, too. Never figured him for the kind of book work that requires, but the guy's clearly ambitious. Anyway, he told me the girl they fished out had a red heart tattooed on one of her butt cheeks. And she had long red hair."

Uh-oh.

"Hair schmair," I said. "How do you know who she is by what's on her ass?"

"How do you think?"

I called on a phrase we all remembered from grammar school when we went to confession and had to tell the priest about anything having to do with thinking about sex.

"I'm having impure thoughts, John."

"Okay, okay." He sat back, suddenly relaxed as if he'd just been hit with a royal flush in a seven-card stud game. "I got involved with her about a year ago. Her name is MaryLou Kowalski. She was a trauma nurse at SF General where we'd taken a perp with a head broken open with a glass ashtray. Twenty-eight and gorgeous."

"The perp?" I said and instantly regretted it as he glared at me. "Sorry," I said again. "Bad joke."

The waiter came and dropped off his new Anchor Steam and shot, and gave me a strange look as he placed a brand-new Chardonnay next to my half-finished one. I hadn't taken my eyes off Johnny.

"Don't tell me," I said.

He nodded and smiled for the first time. "Yeah, the whole disaster. We started seeing each other fairly regularly and it got pretty serious. Sometimes I'd get off shift and there she'd be at my place. Stark naked with two drinks in her hand. Other times she'd call my beeper and name a motel she'd checked into."

Wait a minute. Wait a minute. What's wrong with this picture?

"A motel?" I asked. "What about *her* place?"

"Couldn't," he said evenly.

"*Couldn't?*"

He shrugged, picked up the bottle.

"She was married."

CHAPTER FIVE

Well. Clark Kent redux. I couldn't believe what Johnny was saying, but I didn't want to interrupt his monologue. I wanted to say, "WTF?" as the young folk do nowadays while chatting away on Facebook or some other social media website. But I just shrugged and tipped my head sideways, like friends do when they silently mean *what in the goddam hell were you thinking?*

"Okay," he said, "it started out the usual way. The same old line we used to use. You remember."

I blinked at him. I remembered. "Never failed," I said.

"She could have had any number of doctors or surgeons or whatever, but we just seemed to hit it off. I asked her what time she finished her shift, and she told me. Not like, 'Who are you?' or 'What could you possibly have in mind, Officer?' She simply said, 'Midnight, far end of the ER parking lot.'"

I summoned an iota of enlightenment. "I always wished I looked like you," I said.

Another faint smile.

"So, we got in the car, and I gave her the old routine: 'We have three options: One, we go to some bar and just have a drink. Two, we go right to my place and have the drink. Or three, we go right to *your* place and have the drink.'"

"It always worked for us," I said. Chick magnet, remember?

"Well, it worked like always," Johnny said. "Two chances out of three ain't bad. But listen to this. She then says, 'No, there's a fourth option. We go to your place and *forget* about the drink.'"

"Happier words were never spoken," I opined. Always wanted to use that word. *Opined.* I glommed some Chardonnay. I had suddenly given up pulling.

"So that's how it started," Johnny said, and took a slug of his Anchor Steam and downed his second shot. "We went on from there. Greatest sex I ever had. And she concurred."

Concurred? From a cop?

"So, what's with the married thing?" I asked.

"I don't know. She handled it, I guess. I mean about me. Her husband turned out to be a real asshole and she wanted to leave him. He roughed her up a lot, she said. I never picked up on it. In short order she talked about moving in together, despite our age difference. For chrissakes, she even talked about having kids and scared the piss out of me."

"John. Okay, let's fast-forward. You're screwing a younger married chick, for a year. And she turns up drowned at McCovey Cove? What don't I get here?"

"The husband." He tried to down the shot but it was empty. Instead, he picked up the Anchor Steam and waved again at the waiter. Either I had to start chug-a-lugging my Chardonnay, or—what? Be a man! Refuse a drink.

I asserted my masculinity and waved off the waiter in that "no-no" palm forward sideways half-wave that used to mean "goodbye."

Johnny leaned forward. "He found out about us and went berserk, but when he learned I was a cop he settled down. MaryLou said he threatened to kill her, but, you know, they all say that. However, he beat the shit out of her, instead of me. "

"Of course, that's what they all do," I said. It was all I could think of to say.

I finished one of my drinks and looked at him. Closely. He was a worried man indeed.

"She told me she'd kill herself rather than stay with him. You know the drill. She loved me, and all that."

Chauvinist pig stuff.

I asked, "Did you love her, John?"

"I did," he said. "More than anything, Stevie. I don't know about the 'kids' thing, but yeah. I would have married her."

I melted. I loved this guy and I could see he was tormented by something unsaid.

"But?" It was the most intelligent thing I could think of.

"Well, the reverse. He also said he'd kill *her* if she left him."

I decided on the chug-a-lug option, and it was my turn to wave for another round.

By now it was getting to be Happy Hour and locals started straggling in, taking their usual positions at the bar. The bar attracted what I call the young "computer crowd," the guys who knew software and CGI and all those Adobe and Excel things. The X-Gens or whatever they call themselves. They wore the attire of the day, which meant black suits with skinny legs and no ties. Most carried black computer bags, wore dangling earbuds and no doubt were driving black Teslas or Beemers.

"So, Johnny. My man. You have a girl threatening to kill herself if you don't stay with her and a husband threatening to kill her if you do. We go back a long way, pal. Is there something you're not telling me?"

"You mean, which is it?"

"Like, what the fuck, John?"

"Well, half the force knows about the affair. That's why Bill called me right away. Against regs, but ... you know."

"I know. When did you last see her?"

Like, *hello?* as your granddaughter would day. And, *duh?*

"We had an argument," Johnny said with his head in his hands. "She screamed and screamed and screamed. You know how they do."

I wouldn't touch that one.

"We had a big deal at my place, not violent. More like a Harvard-Yale debate. We defined our 'relationship,' as they call it these days, and 'where was all this going' and all that contemporary crap. Everything seemed to be fine and then, all of a sudden, the husband busts into the place. I hadn't locked the door. I mean, it was like a scene from *Shane*. He's staring daggers, but instead of an axe handle, the guy had a baseball bat. The guy busts into a cop's apartment? And threatens him with a *baseball bat?*"

"Dumb and double dumb," I said.

"So what could I do? Smoke him? Beat the shit out of him? He says he's taking his wife back home and I'm supposed to stop him? He's not breaking any laws because I'm the one fucking his wife, and I'm supposed to say...what? 'Stop, sir. I need to see your ID'?"

"How'd he know you were a cop?"

Johnny shrugged. "I guess she told him, maybe to scare him. So I let him leave," Johnny said morosely. "In order not to embarrass the department."

"Whoa, John. She didn't put up a fight?"

"Sure she did, at first. But I talked her into going with him. Look, I could just see it in the *Chronicle*. 'Cop Beats Up Husband in Love Tryst,' or some shit. So they left and two weeks later she's dragged up at McCovey Cove."

"So, what did you mean on the phone, they think *you* killed her?"

"I probably caused it. It was all my fault to begin with."

"And you think *they think* you killed her...why? To keep it out of the papers? To get rid of her because they'd think it was her husband?"

"I don't know. Something like that. I'm sure he'll be a suspect as well."

"You think he did it?"

"I don't know. She did leave him soon after the scene in my apartment. Hid out in a co-worker's apartment somewhere."

"You got a name for the co-worker?"

He put his head in his hands. "Nah. Lucy somebody." A pause. A heaving sigh. "Christ," he said. His drinker's complexion was shining through now, but when you're Irish a couple beers and shots could do that to you.

I leaned forward. "Johnny, why did you call me? What do you want me to do?"

"I need your help, Stevie. A couple of IA guys showed up and pumped me for an hour."

"Internal Affairs?"

"Yeah. As I said, half the department knew about us."

"They thought you were implicated?"

"They've suspended me," he said.

"That's bullshit," I said.

"Tell me about it. They took my star and gun."

More wine. More beer. "So what do you want me to do?"

"I can't touch it, of course. Ralston's the lead. He's a Homicide Lieutenant now. He already got Commander Perillo's approval. And he's totally on board. I need you to do your own investigation. Working with Bill and his partner, of course, but *sub rosa*."

Nothing like a little Latin to elevate the discussion.

"And Bill's OK with this?"

"Totally. You'll share info with each other."

"Who's his partner?" I asked.

"Young guy named Keene. Harvey, I think."

"You mean like the Detroit Tigers Hall of Famer?"

He shrugged. "I guess so."

I sat back again, thinking. Then, "Where do I start?"

"Bill called me on the way here. There's a new wrinkle."

"Oh?"

"Turns out she didn't drown. She was dead before she hit the water."

CHAPTER SIX

I had met now-Lieutenant Bill Ralston a few times in the old days. He was a rookie uniform then, eager, skinny, full of Dirty Harry justice, but likeable, and as I said, honest. In fact, after a year pulling the requisite traffic cop downtown, he then did patrol for a few years and the last I'd heard about him he was doing something with the vice squad. I'd heard he pulled off a few spectacular collars, like in the movies complete with gunplay and car chases, and got a few medals and commendations. He had the highest compliment from me: He was a good cop. A harder to come by compliment nowadays with some of the officers in the force.

Now, when I met him and his partner outside the main courthouse on Bryant Street, he was a little milder, a little heavier, a recruitment poster model, down to the touch of grey in his Tom Selleck moustache and a fleck of white at his temples. He even wore a conservative blue blazer, white shirt with a button-down collar with just the right degree of flare, a dark blue tie, and tan slacks. He looked like an usher at your Sunday church service.

His partner was a short guy, a bit younger, clean-shaven, and with a darker complexion than you'd expect from a Keene surname. My father always had a sort of embarrassing hobby of guessing the ancestry or nationality of people—like waitresses and waiters, service people, salespeople, and such. Most of the time he'd come close; all of the time it was awkward. He would have guessed Keene's mother was either Italian or of some Middle Eastern ancestry. I made a mental note to ask him sometime.

"Steve Lombardi," Ralston said. "It's been a while."

I shook his proffered hand and slapped him on the shoulder. "It has. How are you, Bill? Congrats on the promo, *Lieutenant.*"

"Thanks," he said, nodding a smile. "Meet my partner, Harvey Keene."

I shook hands with Keene and asked him how many times he got asked for an autograph by a baseball fan. He simply shrugged, smiling. "They mention the name, but they suddenly remember he's much older than me."

"And he's dead," I said.

He nodded, still smiling. "And he's dead."

I was also guessing that Keene spelled his name K-e-e-n-e, the Irish-English way, whereas the ballplayer was K-u-e-n-n, whose parents were Germanic. But I quickly decided to drop it.

Ralston and I did two minutes of catch-up chatter. He was married to a Jewish girl from Brooklyn, had three kids all in grammar school (all raised Catholic according to the marital promise), lived across the bay in Walnut Creek, coached in Little League, was in both a fast-pitch softball league and a bowling league, still attended church on Sundays semi-frequently.

I, in turn, relayed my oh-so-colorful career since leaving the force.

"Man," he said," how many cops play the banjo?"

I laughed, finally said, "Sorry we should meet again on such a weird one."

"You mean Johnny?"

"I mean everything," I said. "What's with the no drowning thing?"

"Wait'll you talk to the M.E. 'Weird' isn't the word for it. How's Johnny doing?"

His tone of voice wasn't quite right. Like, "How's your Aunt Jane doing?" might sound okay if your Aunt Jane was in the hospital after a stroke. But "How's Johnny doing?" sounded more like, "The poor sonofabitch really screwed up, didn't he?"

"Not good," I said. "He knows he's in deep doo-doo and has to keep out of this. That is, *must* keep out. He's been suspended. IA's on his ass."

"I know."

"So, what's the drill here?"

"It gets weirder," he said again. I was getting uncomfortable with how many times the word "weird" was popping up.

"Weirder?" I asked. "How so?"

"Let's just talk with Doctor Feinberg," he said as we all got into his light green Toyota. "Meanwhile, I'll fill you in on what we know about the vic. Johnny told me you're OK with doing your own thing and working with me and Harvey. Share our info."

"*Sub rosa.*"

"What?"

I thought he had a college degree. "Under the table," I said. Then, "So, I got it, we work together. But most cops don't like PIs."

"That's changed a lot lately. You guys can get in places we can't and pry into people's affairs where we can't. Plus, you don't have that damn Miranda restriction."

"That's always been true. But I can't arrest anyone."

He just shrugged. "John said I could trust you implicitly."

"You got it," I said. "I get the feeling we're *both* pulling for John."

He just nodded as he worked the turn onto Van Ness. "We've worked a lot together and I've grown to like him. Like a father figure, maybe."

"He does that to a lot of people. He should have been a priest. So, what have you got on our gal?" I asked.

"Not much yet," he said. "She's originally from a small town in northern Louisiana, population only around seven hundred. Right across the Texas border. Place called Mooringsport, still has some dirt streets, I've heard. Mother died when she was just a kid. Father's an uneducated, often unemployed farmer, Hiram Fitzgerald, but he managed to keep her in school. Bright kid, finally got a scholarship to LSU, where she got her R.N."

"What about the husband?"

"Didn't get much out of him. Some kind of mechanic at the airport. American Airlines. A lawyer shut him up pretty quick. We're running an ID."

We were at the morgue and Ralston was out of the car before he could say much more. Harvey and I followed him.

An autopsy lab is a strange place. First of all, it smells like hell, despite the severe air conditioning system humming in the background. Secondly, it's cold as hell. And I always wondered about that simile—how could something be cold as *hell*? Actually, I always favored cold as a brass monkey or a witch's tits.

Dr. Feinberg, the Medical Examiner, was an affable, small, fat man, bulging stomach with a short necktie that seemed to lie horizontally instead of normally hanging down. He wore the standard white lab coat, and, for reasons nobody apparently had ever asked him, a yellow Scotch-plaid pair of trousers that would have looked better on a British golfer. Of course, he had thick glasses. Every M.E. in America has thick glasses. His outfit notwithstanding, Feinberg had a reputation as a brilliant forensic pathologist. He received his M.D. from Cornell University and did a three-year residency at Cedars Sinai Hospital in Los Angeles, followed by a fellowship at U.C.L.A. He'd been with the City and County of San Francisco for sixteen years, the Chief M.E. for the past four.

After greetings, he led us over to a stainless-steel table and a white sheet that obviously covered a dead body.

"The problem here," he said, "was that they assumed she had drowned when they pulled her out of the water at McCovey Cove."

I said, "Isn't that the normal assumption?"

"Quite," he said.

Cute, I thought. A British movie fan.

"But we found no water in her lungs. No salt water, no fresh water. She didn't drown. Whoever put her in the water knew she was already dead."

"*Put* her in the water?" I said. "What do you mean?"

"I mean just what I said, Inspector. She didn't drown. But she was dead—she couldn't very well put herself in the water. Someone *put* her in the water *after* she was dead. Probably wanted it to *look like* she drowned. What's more, she apparently was murdered."

I looked at Ralston. He looked more upset that the coroner had called me "Inspector" than he was with the conclusion of murder. I decided to let it go; after all, the doc didn't even know who I was. Keene was standing back, just listening; I suspected it was his first autopsy room.

"Doctor, lead me through this. She washes up on shore, obviously drowned, but she *wasn't* drowned. You're saying she was smoked on land and thrown in the drink?"

"Precisely. Some naïve person, or someone panicked out of rationality, wanted it to *look* like she'd drowned."

"How long was she in the water? I mean, could you get a TOD?"

"Too long for me to do a liver temp. So no, we don't have a time of death. All we know is a kid in a kayak going for a home run ball spotted her during a day game, and we're guessing she was put in somewhere during the previous night, for obvious reasons."

"Obvious," I said.

"No witnesses," Ralston said.

"So, when I found no water in her lungs, I immediately went through the complete autopsy. I found no toxics—that means no drugs, no overdoses, no med interactions. But..."

His pause was like an augmented chord at the end of a musical movement. We all stood there in silence, waiting for the next sound.

"I found the most unusual cause of death. She died of a cerebral hemorrhage caused by a brain penetration through her ear canal, probably by something like an ice pick," he said. "Or a knitting needle."

Ralston, Keene and I each looked at each other. "An ice pick?" Keene said before I could.

"Precisely. Someone had penetrated her ear canal with a long sharp object, probably at least six inches long, then withdrew it."

"Ice pick or knitting needle," I mused. "Pretty weird."

"Something long and sharp, at any rate," Dr. Feinberg said. "Her ear drum was completely destroyed."

With Ralston and I still looking at each other, our theatrical doctor poked a finger in the air. "However," he said. "I found some black particles on her ear drum tissue, and a bit more in her ... ah ... brain matter. I'm having them analyzed. I'm sure they're residue from a foreign object."

"My God!" I said. "So she had to be tied up, restrained. You don't approach a person and kill them with an ice pick through the ear."

"Not frontally," Ralston said.

The coroner sat down in a corner of the room and lit a cigarette. The irony of it all was killing me. Oh, sorry. Bad metaphor.

"What's troubling from a forensic standpoint is that such a piercing doesn't necessarily immediately kill a person. She could have lived for a while."

"How long's 'a while'?"

"Maybe an hour or so."

I said, "So you mean she might have been tortured?"

"No, not necessarily. The ice pick, shall we say, went into the upper front portion of her brain. She didn't die right away. She had a hemorrhagic stroke, as I said. Blood flowed into her brain at a rapid rate and she probably went unconscious but died in a matter of an hour or so."

"An hour," I said. "So the killer waited around for her to die before he threw her in the water."

"Seems that way," he said. Feinberg blew a smoke ring and watched it slowly dissipate. Who pays these guys? "If he thought she was dead when he withdrew the object, and he threw her in the water, she would have drowned, yes. Because she would have still been breathing. But ... no water in her lungs? No, he waited for her to die, and *then* put her in the water."

31

"But if he wanted it to look like a drowning, why not throw her in while she was still breathing?"

"Who knows?" the M.E. shrugged. "As I said, panicked people lose all reasoning power."

"So maybe in his panic he knew she was still alive, so he decided to throw her in the bay so she would drown. But she died on the way without his realizing it," Ralston said.

I nodded. Good thought. "Yeah," I said, "he doesn't necessarily sit around for an hour waiting for her to die."

"That too," the doc said. "That too."

"So, Doctor Feinberg. You conclude she was not drowned but was intentionally murdered with a sharp object piercing her brain through her ear canal."

"Precisely," he said.

"Do you conclude anything about her being naked when she washed up?"

"There was only slight evidence of semen in her vagina," he said. "But in the absence of violence—skin under her fingernails, say—I doubt if she was raped. She might have had sexual intercourse shortly before dying."

"Any evidence of her being tied up? Or handcuffed? Anything like that?"

"Apparently, she wasn't restrained and, er, tortured, as you say. There were no signs of ligature of any kind. No other marks on her body. We're thinking she was killed at night, maybe in her sleep."

"Someone snuck up on her," Ralston said.

"Or was sleeping with her," I said. "It sounds to me like she was killed by the guy in bed with her."

"Yes, something like that," the M.E. said. "Or with an arm around her neck. Very close to her, anyway. It had to happen quite suddenly."

"And you're sure she wasn't tied up," I said.

"No. No bruises, either. No sign of violence whatsoever." He shrugged. "Somebody just didn't like her."

I looked again at Ralston, then back at the silent Keene.

No sign of violence?

What the hell do you call getting an ice pick jabbed through your ear?

Chapter Seven

It was the type of day where the heat not only repelled the normal desire for human contact, but replaced it altogether with total bodily celibacy. The sun seemed as if it were suspended at high noon for hours, the threatening heat of a Van Gogh orb of planetary proportions, its rays punishing all two hundred students, parents, and faculty indiscriminately as they sat hostage on the high school's football field. At this point in the field's life cycle, it was made up of mostly dead grass, bare hardpan, linemen's dried blood, and loose, gravelly dirt that crunched under the footsteps of the processing students as they marched in awkward-smiling lockstep toward the stage. No one could remember a hotter day, or at least no memory came to mind that was worse than their current state. The summer of 2010 was gearing up to be more brutal than historically usual, even for this near-desolate part of northern Louisiana.

Everyone hoped for a short ceremony and the promised relief of their car's air conditioner. Especially for one student, the address and closing ceremony couldn't come quickly enough. She could barely wait to grab her diploma and run away from this depressing environment forever. The pretty and shapely young girl with Amy Adams red hair had spent four years of enduring boring lectures, backward classmates, and uninspiring teachers—*"Bueller?... Bueller?... Bueller?"*—all for one final ridiculous charade.

MaryLou Fitzgerald shuffled her feet and changed position for the umpteenth time. She saw it fitting that this final day of high school fell upon such inhospitable weather conditions. She cursed under her breath and thought how ironic it was that the commencement ceremonies were always held at midday—the hottest of hours, in mid-June, the hottest of months. One final intentional abuse of the students, she thought.

The only venue large enough for this event and all the attendees was outdoors, at the North Caddo Magnet High School football field, and on a Saturday such as this, the slim shade made by the few trees behind the goalposts was even more coveted than being named valedictorian.

That latter honor belonged to MaryLou as she sat on the stage looking over the crowd of classmates and faculty for the last time, debating whether to let loose the feelings she had been holding back or if the heat would beat her to the punch. She was perfectly willing to tear her prepared address to shreds and instead tell the whole bunch of pompous phonies—her English class had just completed *Catcher in the Rye*—what she thought of them. But last night she had discussed it with her best friend, an equally bright boy named Cassius Lemoor, whose suitcase now nestled next to hers in the trunk of her ancient Camaro in the parking lot. He had won a baseball scholarship to Tulane and wanted to study either medicine or electrical engineering. Since he'd always had trouble with chemistry, the rightful path was not clear and he hadn't made up his mind. He was now leaning toward the latter because someone had told him he'd never get into medical school unless he had straight A's in chemistry. However, he did have top grades in math and physics. Anyway, after four years of being ostracized for their academic prowess, he and MaryLou were both ready to walk off this stage and never look back.

"And finally, we introduce to you, the Class of 2010, friends and relatives in the audience, your Valedictorian, Miss MaryLou Fitzgerald." The Principal's voice echoed over the makeshift P.A. system as MaryLou sat there immobile with indecision. She so desperately wanted to deliver her scathing rebuke, one she had all but memorized after countless recitations in the shower or in front of the mirror, but as the moment approached, she was losing her courage and whispers of common sense were intruding. She finally stood and walked toward the podium, welcoming the subtle breeze against her face in the humid air. She looked at Cassius, sitting in the front row, and who was slowly, subtly, shaking his head in warning. *Don't do it, MaryLou.*

She opened her mouth, took a deep breath, and exhaled slowly as she cleared her throat, gazing over the crowd. But before she could begin, she was stopped by the sight, in a far back row, of the last person she expected to see.

He had on a ragged straw hat and aviator sunglasses, a blue work shirt with torn sleeves, faded jeans, scuffed brown work boots. He was the only man in the vicinity with a can of beer in his hand, a tall Lone Star. A cloud of tobacco smoke from a long cigarillo hung over her father's head, making the thick air above him look cartoonishly like his own personal pungent cloud. Of all things she was anxious to see in her rearview mirror, her father, Hiram Fitzgerald, was at the top of the list.

Ever since her senior prom.

Even in the torturous heat, she shivered at the memory.

Most of her friends knew that she and Cassius were close pals, but she carefully kept it from her father. Her brother Ethan was also a close friend of Cassius, and he understood the need for secrecy. The whole town knew that such was Hiram Fitzgerald's racism that he even refused to drink from public water fountains since segregation was reluctantly outlawed decades after President Johnson had signed the Civil Rights Act back in 1964.

So it was that Hiram had no knowledge of Cassius being MaryLou's date for the prom. When he asked, she had told him she had no date, that she was just driving herself to the gym and would join a bunch of the other dateless girls. It was more like a mixer, she explained, and her sorority of the dateless would make do and enjoy the evening together.

But for all his intense bigotry, Hiram was no dope. He sensed something not quite right. He knew MaryLou was one of the most attractive girls in the parish, as well as one of the brightest, and he couldn't quite fathom that no boys had asked her to be their escort to the prom. So, after an early evening drinking at his local saloon hangout, Hiram decided to drive over to the high school gym, his can of Lone Star in hand, and take a peek into the festivities.

He crept along a tree line at one side of the gym and stopped next to a rickety tin shed that held the school's red-and-black sports uniforms and various pieces of equipment. A row of windows along the side of the gym was low enough to peer in.

And when he did, Hiram Fitzgerald blew up.

Inside, a small band was playing softly and dozens of couples were awkwardly dancing across the gym boards. A row of girls without dance partners sat along a far wall, and close to Hiram's window, a group of boys were sneakily smoking cigarettes. He eyed the couples carefully, at first not seeing MaryLou, until her flashing red hair came into view and hit Hiram like a torpedo.

Her hand was being held by a Black hand and her cheek was resting lightly against a Black cheek.

Hiram threw his beer can into the bushes and raced around to the front of the gym. He crashed through the front doors, past a startled pair of girls at a greeting table, and ran through equally startled pairs of young dancers.

"You son of a bitch!" he roared. The band stopped abruptly. Alarmed kids looked around, wondering who he was and who he was yelling at.

He rushed up to MaryLou and a shocked Cassius. "Get your fucking hands off her!"

"Dad, no!"

Hiram broke between them and shoved Cassius away with such force that the boy stumbled backwards and fell against a long utility table. The red-faced Hiram turned and grabbed MaryLou by the wrist and jerked her around. "You little bitch!" She fell to her knees and he began dragging her until she regained her balance. But she fell again and he kept dragging her behind him as he headed for the door. It was all she could do to get back on her feet.

"Dad stop!" she screamed. Other girls were screaming around her. The boys looked around, not knowing what to do. Cassius hesitantly followed Hiram toward the door.

A pair of male chaperones suddenly appeared and blocked Hiram's way. They were both younger than Hiram, neatly dressed in slacks, open-necked business shirts, and blazers.

"Mister Fitzgerald—"

"Get the fuck out of my way! I'm taking my daughter home!"

One of the chaperone fathers stepped toward him.

"Just a second, Hiram! You can't—"

Hiram stiff-armed him backward with another epithet and bullied his way past the helpless on-lookers, yanking MaryLou through the doors. One of the chaperones cursed, took off his jacket and started after Hiram with clenched fists. The second chaperone grabbed him and held him back.

"Let him go, Pete. He ain't worth it."

Pete settled down, cursed again, and went back to find his jacket.

MaryLou was now sobbing and lost her footing again as he spotted her car and shoved her toward it. He threw her in the back seat, locked the doors and sped away as she cried her heart out behind him.

She shuddered again. She couldn't remember saying five words to him since. The embarrassment followed for the rest of the term, and she felt even close friends behaving more coolly around her. When Cassius's father heard about the skirmish, he confronted his son, who told him about it but vigorously kept his father from driving to Mooringsport and forcefully confronting Hiram. Of course, Cassius had been totally devastated and shared MaryLou's mortification. From then until graduation they carefully kept their relationship—which she steadfastly kept wholly platonic—but continued only under careful circumspection.

MaryLou began the speech almost hypnotically fixated on her father. She glanced down, turning over the prepared pages, worn and wrinkled now from excessive rewriting, and looked up again. Her father was gone. As the words tumbled mechanically from her mouth, she couldn't help but think how typical it would be for him not to give a damn what she had to say.

Why was he there in the first place?

Before long she was concluding her address and thanking the very people she had promised herself to condemn.

She couldn't wait to get away from not just the school and the stinking farm she was raised on, but also the entire parish in general and the few, but loud, bigoted citizens of Mooringsport and nearby Caddo Lake, which ironically was the birthplace a century ago of the legendary Black folk singer known as Huddie "Leadbelly" Ledbetter. She smiled as she thought how the town has been so historically resistant to change that it couldn't keep, neither in location nor in memory, its most talented native son, the self-anointed "King of the 12-string guitar" and composer of such hits as" Rock Island Line" "Cotton Fields Back Home," and "Good Night, Irene."

Now she couldn't wait to make the four-hour drive to Baton Rouge, where she would begin her first scholarship semester at LSU's celebrated School of Nursing, earning her B.S.N. and then move to California, specifically to San Francisco, the farthest place she could find on the map from Mooringsport. Well, other than rainy Seattle. In fact, she had applied for an early summer course, not so much out of anxiety to begin academics early, but was unable to stand another two months of summer in some of the grimmest environments in America. Even her older brother Ethan had lied about his age and enlisted in the Navy the day after he turned seventeen to escape the harshness of their farming life.

The farm her father and grandfather had earned as some of the few white indentured servants in Louisiana was a mile from Mooringsport and Caddo Lake, not far from the Texas border. It was thirty-two and one-half acres, most of it cleared for cotton and corn, and the rest still heavily wooded with long- and short-needle pine trees. A dirt road riddled with potholes split the property in two and then swung westward toward Leigh, Texas.

MaryLou and her brother were raised by Hiram after their mother died of pneumonia when they were four and three years old, respectively. They lived in a cabin built of grey planking and set atop three-foot sections of footing hewn out of the trunk of an oak tree, protection against the occasional flood. A front porch ran the length of the cabin, supported by an overhanging roof of corrugated tin. In the back was a small garden with a well, an awful smelling outhouse, a chicken coop, a rabbit hutch, two sows, and a Guernsey. Throughout grammar and high school, MaryLou and Ethan were expected to bear their burden of farming and livestock chores until it became too dark to work and they could gulp down dinner and tend to their homework after they cleared the table. Hiram usually commandeered the small parlor, where he was either stretched out drunk or watching silly game shows on a small black-and-white TV.

The kids hated every minute of their youth.

She finished her speech and the audience applause snapped her out of her trance-like state, and before she knew it, she was shaking the Principal's hand while receiving her diploma—her ticket to freedom. Without waiting for the conclusion of the ceremony, MaryLou sped down the steps, tore off her cap and gown, and raced in the tank top and jean cutoffs she had on underneath across the football field like so many Rebels fullbacks and wide receivers did before her, and toward her waiting car and both hers and Cassius' pre-packed luggage.

CHAPTER EIGHT

The biggest thrill of young MaryLou's life came at her next graduation, four years later when her best friend Cassius affixed her nursing school pin to her uniform on the vast LSU parade ground. Things were suddenly happening quickly. Just last week she watched Cassius receive his B.S. in Electrical Engineering degree at Tulane, graduating *magna cum laude*. Now, here at LSU, he was watching her fulfill her dream. Cassius had already been recruited by a prominent semiconductor firm in Austin, and eager to leave Louisiana once and for all, she agreed to drive him to Austin and then drive to San Francisco in search of her own Gold Rush; she had been accepted by San Francisco General Hospital as a trauma nurse in the emergency department. She was scheduled to take her tests for California R.N. licensing in three weeks.

The distance from Baton Rouge to Austin was almost 500 miles and Cassius suggested they not try to make it in one drive. Besides, the R. N. pinning ceremony lasted until three p.m. and neither of them wanted to drive all night.

"Let's make it just past Lafayette and get a decent night's sleep," MaryLou said as she cranked over the ignition.

"And a decent dinner," Cassius said. "I've been eating with my roommates all week."

"Deal," she said. "I hear it's a pretty town."

"I had a classmate from there," he said. "He always claimed Lafayette's where you went if you wanted to see the *real* bayou."

"Not New Orleans?"

"He said canoeing down the swamp under the willows drooping with Spanish moss is an unforgettable experience."

"What about alligators," she said.

"I guess you beat them off with the paddle."

She smiled and shrugged. "Whatever."

He slapped her knee. "Anyway, we're free at last, free at last. Great God almighty, we're free at last!"

She laughed. "Where have I heard that before?"

"An Ava DuVernay movie?"

She laughed again. Swerving onto the road past the Mississippi River on the right she saw the signs indicating highway U.S. 10 west toward Texas. They both leaned back and breathed easily.

They were on their way.

MaryLou and Cassius were glad Tulane and LSU were only about 80 miles from each other, an hour and a half drive. Sometimes, when she drove to Tulane, he would drive her back to LSU and she'd let him take her car back. In effect, although they were in different colleges, they owned the same car.

They had attended Green Wave and Tigers football and basketball games, he in his light green and dark green shirts and jacket, she resplendent in her purple and yellow gear. They had occasional dinners, too, went to movies, and every now and then a picnic on the lake. Not really dates, MaryLou insisted, although she always knew Cassius had retained a romantic interest in her ever since high school. She'd had to rebuke him a few times, but always careful to be as tender and understanding as possible. When she was honest with herself, she had to admit an erotic arousal on her part, especially when kissing goodnight, but she'd become adept at quickly suppressing it. She had dated a few other men in college, when she'd had the time, but nothing serious. San Francisco was her ultimate goal and she didn't want to get involved with anyone in Louisiana.

Cassius had told her he also had dated a few women at Tulane, but always with the codicil that they weren't "quite right." MaryLou knew what that was code for, and couldn't help blushing. Anyway, she was proud of her independence and, to his eternal frustration, had reminded him of it on several occasions.

Now, as she hit Interstate 10 heading northwest to the Texas capitol, she was acutely aware there would have to be a discussion about the overnight sleeping arrangements in Lafayette.

But that could wait until later.

CHAPTER NINE

I thought about what was going on. Ralston had told me that before the husband had lawyered up, they grilled him, of course, the first "person of interest," as they say these days. Apparently, he had an alibi, albeit a weak one: the girl had stormed out of their house after a rough-and-tumble argument and he had gone down to the local pub to drown his sorrows. When he came home, she was still gone and he hadn't seen hide nor hair of her for the two weeks until she was found. He tried to see her at the hospital a few times but she refused to come out and meet him. She cautioned personnel at the entrance reception that under no circumstance did she want any contact with him. On the occasions when he became insistently belligerent, they had to call security to escort him from the premises.

Then his lawyer showed up.

I should talk with him, I thought—I didn't have the dumb Miranda encumbrance. It always bugged me that we had to inform a guy of his rights when we'd just caught him red-handed slicing someone's throat with seven eye-witnesses signing up to ID the sonofabitch. I always figured he forfeited his rights when he decided to become a monster.

Okay, I'll talk to the husband. Then what? Suspects? I figured if she was found in McCovey Cove during a ball game, there were forty-one thousand suspects. Another sellout crowd.

Maybe the hospital. Did anyone there dislike her enough to waste her? A patient? A competitive nurse? A supervisor? And, I thought as I almost cut myself shaving, maybe she was humping somebody other than Johnny Lynch. It wasn't out of the realm of possibility that she was secretly dating a co-worker who had become psychotically enraged when she broke off the relationship. And for that matter, without John knowing it she could have been screwing the whole damn hospital staff!

But there we go again. According to Ralston, the husband was no dope. If she were banging the entire University of California Medical School Alumni Association, something would have happened before now. And I had to think my old buddy Lynch would certainly not have been taken in by Miss Promiscuous Trollop, R.N.

Or would he?

As the wise old Socrates said in the Forum to the eager young Plato while ankle-biter Aristotle crawled around the sand at their feet, "You never know."

CHAPTER TEN

I decided not to warn him by calling and to just show up at the front door. Which I did.

It was a quiet working-class neighborhood in Belmont, one of the last such in the ever-gentrifying SF Bay Area. The town is a southern San Francisco suburb of about twenty-five thousand not far from the airport and sprawling up toward the hills to the west. They say the town got its name from the Italian "*bel monte*," meaning "beautiful mountain," but most Bay Area residents don't even notice the hill it is named for right off the 101 freeway just south of the airport. The mountains behind it might be beautiful, but Belmont was largely plain.

I'd done some checking and knew Walter Kowalski had married MaryLou Fitzgerald, R.N. four years ago. He was an aircraft engine inspector for American Airlines, no police record, one speeding ticket when he was a sophomore at San Francisco State University. Native San Franciscan, born and raised in the Portola District, an uneventful four years at Balboa High, never did graduate from SF State. Ralston called him "Clean as a whistle."

Except we knew he liked to beat up women.

It was ten in the morning when I got there. There was nothing special about the house—one story tract house, maybe fifty years old, once stylish. Gray tongue-in-groove siding with black trim, shingle roof, small front yard ringed by box hedges, a neglected orange tree, and a narrow concrete walk to the front door. There was a pink-and white-chalked hopscotch grid on the sidewalk where kids were playing and farther down the street a group of boys played what looked like a stickball game. I guessed the house at two bedrooms, one-and-a-half baths, maybe a small breakfast nook and a larger dining table in a corner of the living room. I went up the three wooden entrance steps and rang the bell.

Nothing. I rang again and looked back at the red Ford Escape in the driveway.

Still nothing. This time I rapped on the door glass with my heavy gold Notre Dame ring. I wanted anyone hiding at home to know I wasn't going away.

Now I heard a few heavy steps inside and suddenly the door yanked open.

He said nothing, leaning on the frame, but his look told me he was surprised at my age. He was a big guy, lots of curly black hair, a bushy goatee of the same color, and hazel eyes. Without the goatee and with a decent haircut he was probably quite a handsome dude. His otherwise unremarkable face was punctuated with a black eye.

He was dressed in white coveralls with the American Airlines logo on the breast pocket. He was either getting ready to go to work or just got home.

"Mister Kowalski?"

"Yeah?" Confused. Maybe he thought I was a Depends salesman.

I flashed my ID card. "Steve Lombardi. I'm a private investigator working on the MaryLou Kowalski case. May I ask you a few questions?"

Immediately he grabbed the doorknob and started to slam the door. My foot stopped it.

"I already talked to the cops. My lawyer told me not to talk to no one anymore."

"He probably told you not to talk to any more cops. I'm not a cop." Then, as pleasantly as I could, "So you won't be breaking your promise to the lawyer."

"I'll be breaking your foot if you don't get it out of the doorway," he said.

"Just a few questions. Please?" I thought I could placate him by adding, "My, that's a nasty shiner. An accident?"

"None of your business. Listen buddy. This is a private residence and you're breaking the law. Get your fucking foot out, *now!*"

"Wow, there's certainly a lot of 'breaking' going on," I said. He was right, of course, but I wasn't budging. But then he raised his booted foot and was about to bring it down on my toes when I swiftly withdrew.

I was fighting the temptation to thrust out my flat palm in a nanosecond and shove his bully nose up into his skull, but while I thought about my subsequent jail time the door slammed with a force I expected to shatter the glass pane.

The proverbial dead end. I knew it would do no good to interrogate him with his lawyer present. I would have to rely on the police report from their interrogation of Kowalski as a person of interest. Ralston could get me a copy. I also made a mental note to ask him about Kowalski's black eye.

On the way back to my car I checked out the Ford. A *Guns and Ammo* magazine on the front seat, next to a discarded Golden Arches soda cup. A few canvas shopping bags and a red six-pack wine carrier on the back seat. There were also two empty beer cans on the floor.

And the tires were covered with mud.

CHAPTER ELEVEN

MaryLou was nervous. Her stomach felt as though she had left it back in Baton Rouge even though she was dozens of miles west at this point, driving across the Texas state line with Cassius. As they entered the quaint town of Orange and she first saw the big green sign saying "Welcome to Texas. Drive friendly – the Texas way" she felt the thrill all the way down to her heels. It was the first time she had been outside of Louisiana, save for that one exception when she drove with some friends to watch her beloved LSU football team play Mississippi State in Starkville. However, she had drunk more during that trip than any other time in her life combined. It was why she barely recalled anything from that excursion besides the smell of vomit and the sound of trumpets, so that trip really doesn't count, she told herself.

"Nice sign," she said gleefully. Since Cassius insisted on driving to their first stop that left MaryLou in the passenger seat barely playing co-pilot—she was more a captive audience than a partner in their navigation to Austin. In fact, MaryLou was nervous about their destination. Not San Francisco; she couldn't wait to get there. She'd been dreaming about leaving her home state behind in favor of the cosmopolitan Bay Area since she could remember. No, she was nervous about whatever motel they'd arrive at to spend the night because they couldn't afford two rooms.

Cassius was nice enough, MaryLou wasn't afraid of that, but was nervous for the talk she knew she would inevitably have to have with him regarding the sleeping arrangement. They had always been close, even in college they hardly went more than a few weekends without seeing each other. And MaryLou was thrilled to have Cassius at her graduation, to have someone from back home see her accomplishments and share in her pride for being able to leave Louisiana. She didn't care about her father, and her brother Ethan was away in the Navy.

However, Cassius's "like" was always more intensely romantic than her more platonic "like" for him. That is, his overall demeanor seemed to have a more amorous aura to it, however subtle. It was a feeling she had known for a while, but always hoped would fade away as they each began to lead more independent lives. Sure, he had dated girls while at Tulane, and she even went out with a few of his friends when they visited her at LSU, but she had kept her side of it strictly platonic. His side always gave her a feeling that always lingered, an unspoken implication that he expected them to be together once their separate schooling was over.

Now, with Austin and San Francisco being much farther apart than Tulane and LSU, MaryLou knew this future could only be a fantasy. If only Cassius had the same realization. Was she being realistic? She debated when would be the best time to bring this up. Surely it would have to be before they arrive at the front desk and Cassius asks for a room with a single bed, and MaryLou would need to correct the reservation right there on the spot. That would be too embarrassing for Cassius; she couldn't do that to him. But as the miles ticked on, she still couldn't bring herself to broach the subject. She sat there in silence, during what should be a relaxing journey. Like much of her life, there always seemed to be one more obstacle before she could be happy.

"So, how long do you think it'll take you to get to Frisco from Texas?" Cassius asked.

It was a harmless enough question and snapped MaryLou out of her trance.

"Oh, I don't know, maybe another three days. I'll stay on Highway 10 to San Diego, then straight up I-5. Or maybe three or four more days and try to see some sights," she responded. "I was thinking of taking another route and stopping by the Grand Canyon on my way for a bit, maybe even see Yosemite. Who knows when I'll get the chance again?"

"That sounds nice. We've sure never seen anything like those places where we're from," he added.

"No," she thought. "No, we haven't."

The sun had barely set when the glittering lights of the approaching roadside shops, services, motels and restaurants flickered on. They passed a Ramada Inn on their left, the marquee welcoming a sales convention from Dallas.

"No vacancy. Welcome Peterbilt Dealers. Hmmmm." She read aloud from a reader board below the neon marquee, relieved to get at least a few more minutes before broaching the subject of their room. "Are they telling Peterbilt dealers that they're welcome but there's no vacancy?"

"I think they're telling us there's no vacancy unless we're Peterbilt dealers."

She laughed. "Cassius, remember that time we played hooky from school, and we ran past the parking lot toward Ms. Molly's car?"

Cassius smirked. It was a funny question coming right out of the blue. They'd known each other for so long, these stories were told much the same way an old married couple would—retold for their own delight at listening to the other talk and pass the time.

"Yeah, and she caught me hiding behind the dumpster, but you got away and were able to spend the whole day in Shreveport. Man, the principal really laid into me that day."

"But you didn't tell them where I was," she interjected. "That was one of the best days of my life."

"Well I'm glad you had fun, but you also didn't have to wash the lockers in that heat for the next two weekends," he quipped back.

"No," she said, "I didn't, but just the freedom of being alone. That's what I meant. Not having to answer to anyone, even for one day. No one knew me there, or even where I was."

"Didn't you get that in college?" Cassius asked.

"Not really, because I always had teachers, or assignments, work, just responsibilities."

"Well, we'll always have that. You do appreciate that you're on your way to a real job in California, right? As much as they might say people are different out there, everyone has to work."

"Yeah," she trailed off. "But not during this drive. Once I drop you off, I'll be free as a bird." She stared out into the highway, watching the headlights buzz past her, like memories that haven't happened yet—new adventures coming at her, and will soon be in the rear-view mirror as quickly as they appeared.

She continued, "I'm excited to start over. New faces, new opportunity, nothing from my past holding me back."

"I didn't realize I was holding you back," Cassius said, looking at her. He was trying to bring her back to reality. MaryLou would get in these moods, where she would wish that everything from her past would disappear. He would fight to keep her grounded, to keep himself in her life. It was a battle that he was just realizing he might never win.

Desperate to change the subject, Cassius spotted a glowing sign up ahead.

"Bayou Bed and Breakfast" he read aloud. He put on his blinker and began to pull over.

"Looks like as good a place as any," he stated.

MaryLou nodded. She knew this place was no accident. A bed and breakfast screams romance, not a simple motel for friends.

CHAPTER TWELVE

The crunch of the gravel as their creaky old Camaro slowed to a halt was the only noise in the early evening. The hum of the highway barely audible through the trees, the gravel echoing through the air like crickets might on one of those long summer nights near Caddo Lake—a kind of reminiscence that signaled how alone they were on the highway.

"Cassius," she started. "Before we go in there, I want to let you know upfront we should get our own beds for the night. I just want us to be friends and not have anything weird happen or complicate our feelings before you settle in Texas and I go to California."

He looked back at her, feigning puzzlement over what she was saying. He was not hiding his combination of shock at her bluntness and disappointment in her decision as well as he thought he was.

He put on a brave face. "Well yeah," he started. "I'm not sure where you interpreted any other motives happening here. I mean we've bunked together now and then our whole lives and throughout college without ever needing to bring this up, but okay."

"Well, I know how you feel," she said. "I just don't want you to feel … I don't know. Rejected?"

"But I do feel. You know I'm mad about you, Mary."

She reached over and held his hand. "I just want you to understand. I'm just not ready …"

He quickly withdrew his hand from hers. "That's fine, but if that's the case you can't go doing stuff like that." He looked down at their hands.

"Cassius …"

He got out of the car and closed the door harder than he needed to—even though the car was old and some extra effort was often required to get it to do anything. He started walking up to the front door, the crunch of the gravel beneath his boots rather than the tires now capitalizing the silence.

MaryLou got out and followed him, noticing he hadn't bothered to hold the door open for her as he usually did. She walked into the lobby several steps behind him. He was already chatting with the man behind the counter.

"But we'll only be staying the one night." Cassius explained.

"Sorry," the man replied, "but since we haven't had many visitors these past few weeks, I let our maid take the week off, so we only have four rooms that have been serviced and are ready for guests, and none of them have two beds. Just the single queen available. There's a Ramada Inn up the road."

"That's sold out," Cassius said.

"Oh yeah, I forgot. Big convention, I hear," the man said, shrugging.

Cassius looked at MaryLou. Followed by the man behind the counter. Both were waiting on her to make up her mind. Is she really the type of girl who would make them get back in the car and cruise around half the night looking for another lodging just because there are no two-bed rooms available? Especially when Cassius was right, they had spent the night in the same bed countless times before and besides the occasional spooning—which half of the time she was just as guilty of as Cassius—nothing had happened.

She felt the pressure now and spoke up, curtly. "It's been a long day, let's just take the room. I mean we're already here." She tried to sound nonchalant and play the "cool" girl part, but they both felt the response empty.

Cassius turned back to the clerk. "Well, we'll take the queen room for the night then."

They completed the transaction and less than fifteen minutes later they both were lying exhausted on the bed, this time no gravel to mask the silence between them.

❧ ❧ ❧

The Bayou Bed and Breakfast was a two-story wooden structure that looked like it had been established in the early twentieth century and had not had any major renovations and only minor cosmetic upgrades and furnishings since that time. It would surprise MaryLou to learn the next morning that the building was only thirty years old—the repeated flooding from hurricanes and constant humidity ages every wooden building in southern Texas the same way.

The room consisted of a small TV with two rabbit-ear antennas, but one broken ear so it looked more like Alfalfa from the Little Rascals than a rabbit, and a small nightstand, with the expected copy of the Gideon Bible in the top drawer. The curtains hung in such a way that most of the side portions of the window were covered, but even when expanded to their max, they would not cover the entire window. This wasn't a problem now, but surely would be in the morning when the sun would find any crack to shine in and wake its guests. Besides the dingy bathroom, the last piece of furniture was the bed. Without any chair or table, it made itself the only place to relax in the room—there was no place for her to hide, avoiding Cassius was going to be impossible.

Cassius was now upright on the foot of the bed, trying his best to get any signal he could from the television. After positioning Alfalfa's hair in such an angle that Cassius contorted a moment's clear reception of the local news network, it was quickly lost to the snowy static again. He gave up and turned to her at the head of the bed.

"I thought this place would be nicer when I read the sign saying 'Bed and Breakfast.' It's just another roadside motel. Guess their marketing worked, huh?"

She looked around, "It's not all bad. I mean, we'll hit the sack and be out of here before sun-up."

He smirked. MaryLou always had a retort to everything.

MaryLou got up and started making it obvious she was getting ready for bed. Cassius asked, "Hey, it's still our graduation weekend.

Feel like celebrating at all? I'm sure we can get a drink back at that Ramada."

It was starting, she thought to herself. The cocktail preliminaries, she called it. "No, I'm just beat, honestly. It's been a long trip already and I'm barely a state removed from where we started. I think I'm going to brush my teeth and turn in." She grabbed her small valise and stepped into the bathroom and shut the door.

MaryLou brushed her teeth, but slowly, and pausing often to crane and try to hear what Cassius was doing in the other room. She wasn't hiding, she told herself. She was getting ready for bed—just more slowly than normal and with the fear that any noise she made might trigger a response. Walking on eggshells? Try walking around a scorned man.

She heard the door open and close and after a minute popped her head out of the bathroom, slowly. He was gone. She parted the shades of the room and peered out the window into the night. In the neon glow she saw the car was leaving the parking lot. He must have left in search of a drink himself. Relieved, she put on her pajamas and slid into the bed, turning off the light and facing the wall so she could act like she was asleep when he returned.

CHAPTER THIRTEEN

I sat at the end of the bar in my favorite saloon, the 2 A.M. Club in Mill Valley, and nursed a very nice Buena Vista Chardonnay with my two slices of pepperoni pizza. I had been thinking about wife-beater Kowalski and his belligerent attitude, and about the muddy wheels on his Ford. Did it mean anything? This being August, it hadn't rained in months. But so what? There are lots of muddy spots all around: golf courses, Golden Gate Park, creeks, boat launches, beaches...

Boat launches and beaches? As in, places to dump dead bodies in the bay?

I hadn't thought about it before, but I suddenly wondered whether finding a washed-up body at Point A, could be traced to having entered the water at Point B. And what role would the tides play? In other words, could it be shown with relative accuracy that our MaryLou at McCovey Cove was dumped into the bay at, say, Tiburon, a few miles across the water?

I decided to visit the Bay Model in Sausalito.

The Bay Model is a fascinating place. Built and operated by the Army Corps of Engineers soon after World War Two, the model is a 1.5-acre three-dimensional representation of the waterways of the entire San Francisco Bay region. By virtue of an elaborate system of pumps and drains throughout 286 five-ton concrete slabs, it accurately simulates tides, currents, river inflows and other variables. One can walk the entire model and watch, at hip level, tidal activity in any coastal town or bayside site all around the bay and nearby delta. And the clarity of the water and three-dimensionality of it all lets you see how deep the water is at any point, from the plunging channel directly under the Golden Gate Bridge, to the colorful salt flats to the south, and finally north to the shallows of Corte Madera Creek and the Napa River.

I checked the time and before long I was navigating the alleys and narrow turns through Sausalito's shoreline and finally pulled into the Bay Model parking lot. At the entrance, I was greeted by a pleasant uniformed guy, given a brochure, and invited to a seven-minute video show about the Bay Area's "delicate" waterway system. I always cringe when I hear those terms from oh-so-sensitive citizens concerned about the "delicate" environment and "fragile" planet. I'm tempted to ask them how the hell the "fragile" planet survived meteor crashes, floods, earthquakes, innumerable volcanoes, ice ages, and other calamities and still remained our beautiful blue marble. I am reminded that the earth wasn't hospitable during those eras of tectonic change either, so touché.

I skipped the video show and casually walked around the model. It was chilly and quiet. The model was working and the water flowed quietly with the tides, which I noted were unusually high and low for this time of year. I walked past the Marin county markers—each town and geographic feature was marked by a small sign identifying it—past the Golden Gate Bridge, past the Marina and came to the Bay Bridge and Oracle Park. I examined McCovey Cove and surrounding piers closely.

Now what? I looked eastward across the Bay toward Treasure Island, then looked left, northward, toward Alcatraz and then southward toward the airport and the San Mateo Bridge. But what was I seeing? I needed a guide of some kind.

I retraced my steps back to the entrance and approached Uniformed Guy again.

"Is there a hydrologist or some tidal expert I could talk to?"

"We don't have a scientific staff," he said. "Budget cuts and all. But maybe Ranger Kaufman can help you."

"Great," I said. "Where can I find him?"

"I'll go get her," he said. "She may be conducting a tour."

I nodded a thank you. Him was a her.

After a few minutes Uniformed Guy came back with a short, pretty, dark-haired woman in a green U.S. Forest Service uniform, which she filled out nicely. I guessed she was in her twenties. And as a guy who loves women in uniform, I was quite impressed.

"Hi, I'm Sandy," she said. "How can I help you?"

"I have a question about the tides," I said, nodding toward the Bay Model entrance. "Can I show you something?"

"Surely."

"Follow me," I said. I didn't want Uniformed Guy to hear what I was going to tell her.

As she followed me through the video room and back to the McCovey Cove site, I briefly told her who I was, what I was doing, and what I wanted to know. "So," I concluded, "is it possible to tell where a washed-up body first entered the water?"

We were at the site and I reached over and pointed with a long pencil to where the Kowalski girl had been found. Ranger Kaufman had a serious look on her face. I had thought at first that she might not have believed me, but now I knew better. She carefully looked north, and then south, then over to Treasure Island, then back to the Marin Headlands.

"Well," she said with a sigh, putting her hands on her hips. "I'm not a hydrologist, mind you, but I can give you an educated guess."

"Please do," I said.

"I'd say there are two scenarios: tide coming in and tide going out. Slack tide wouldn't move her at all." She looked left again. "If the tide were coming in and she entered the bay at Fort Point under the bridge, say, or somewhere along the Marina, then she'd have to drift past a lot of piers and other projections, then past the Ferry Building and the ferry landing, then down farther under the Bay Bridge, past a few more marinas, and make a hard-right turn into McCovey Cove."

She shook her head slowly. "Not likely. Way too far, way too much blockage."

I nodded.

Now she looked right. "And if the tide were coming out, and she entered the bay somewhere south of the cove, say around Belmont..."

Belmont? A coincidental reference to where Bully Kowalski lived?

"...then she'd have to drift around the airport, around Candlestick Point, around another marina and a lot of other projections into the bay, and make a hard *left* into the cove." She exhaled. "Also not likely, for all the same reasons."

I nodded again. "What about across the bay, or over around Tiburon?"

She shook her head. "No, tide going out, she'd go right under the Golden Gate Bridge, and tide coming in, she'd probably end up on the East Bay shoreline somewhere, probably Oakland."

She paused while I thought about it.

"I'm afraid I'm not being much help, am I?"

"No, that's a great help," I hastened to say. "It gives me a few ideas. Thank you so much."

"If you want my two cents worth," she said hesitantly, "from what you've told me, I'd say she was dumped in right off the 3rd Street Bridge, what they call the Lefty O'Doul Bridge. Right directly into McCovey Cove."

"Thanks," I said again.

She shook my hand and left me to my thoughts.

So, the odds were really long that she'd been put in the water very much further south or north of McCovey Cove. Which made me think that our killer didn't drive a helluva long way to dump her. In fact, the odds were getting greater that she *was* actually dumped off the bridge right near Oracle Park.

Which made me think he lived in the city.

And, it now occurred to me, why was I thinking he was a "he?"

Jealousy, anyone?

CHAPTER FOURTEEN

MaryLou awoke with a sense of panic. Although she was facing the wall it was already bright enough to make her think it was mid-morning. Those damn drapes, she thought to herself. Since she chose the side of the bed against the wall, she couldn't crane her head around to see the time without waking Cassius.

He had apparently come in at some point last night when she was asleep, more soundly than she expected she'd be. She thought she sniffed alcohol; maybe he'd tied one on and passed out right next to her. They weren't touching, however, maybe a couple of inches or so between them.

As MaryLou slipped out of bed at the bottom end as quietly as she could, her joints and lower back felt sore. Must be this old mattress, she surmised. She glanced over at Cassius, still facing away from where she had been lying, wearing only his boxer shorts. MaryLou, however, had slept in her full pajamas. She glanced at the clock as she made her way to the bathroom. It read 6:54 a.m.

MaryLou closed the door softly behind her, turning the knob carefully so as not to click it shut. As the lights flickered on, she saw the bathroom was in much more disarray than she'd left it. The window had been left open and the sound of the highway was already buzzing. There were towels on the floor, and the sink and counter were strewn with toothpaste, lotion, mini shampoos, and a condom package ripped at the corner, but with the condom still unused in the package.

She sighed. She's almost on her own. Just a few more hours to Austin, then she was really able to start her road trip. MaryLou had begun cleaning up the towels and items on the counter while daydreaming of the places she would visit on her way to California when Cassius knocked on the door.

"Hey," he said, muffled. "Can I get in there? I gotta go!"

"Sure," she responded. She glanced at herself in the mirror briefly, running her fingers through her hair trying to fix herself up as quickly as possible and opened the door.

They slid by each other quickly, she pulling the door closed. Cassius had opened the curtain and the full strength of the sun's morning rays filled their small room, bringing out an even yellower stain to the already faded wallpaper. Soon she heard the toilet flush, then water running. It turned off and he whipped the door open.

"What's with the mess in here?" he asked her.

"How should I know? I went to bed; you were the one who came in late."

"Yeah, but I only brushed my teeth."

MaryLou looked confused. "Weren't you out drinking last night?"

"I only had a couple drinks. I went out to this bar a ways up the road and got a few beers. I met some guy there and when I told him we had just graduated and I was driving to Texas and you to San Francisco. He bought me one more for the road before he took off. I came right back."

"Only a few?"

Cassius continued. "I mean I was driving, I had to park a little crooked when I got in cause some piece of shit in a beat-up blue Trans Am was parked in two spots. Anyway, just come grab everything in here that's yours and we can pack up and get going."

She glanced outside. His car was parked off-center slightly, but she also thought he may just be trying to cover up for the embarrassment of the condom he left out.

MaryLou furrowed her brow. "So…maybe more than a few, then?"

Cassius looked sheepish. "Well, I figured I had nothing better to do."

MaryLou forced a laugh. "You mean with the TV broken, and all…"

Cassius put on his contrite look she'd seen a few times before. "Well, I mean… uh…"

She cut him off. "Forget it, Cassius. No harm done. Get dressed. We'll eat and get on the road."

She dashed into the bathroom, quickly cleaned up all the toiletries, and left the condom right where she found it, in plain sight for him to see. She then left the bathroom door open for him, jammed all her stuff into her valise, threw it on the bed and went out the door.

"Meet you outside," she said.

After a quick banana, some quiche, a small glass of tomato juice and coffee, they went back to the room to fetch their stuff and use the bathroom once more. He didn't mention the condom package and never acknowledged the smirk on her face. But just before she opened the door, he grabbed her suddenly by the waist, spun her around and kissed her. Roughly at first, then softer and she let herself melt into him, returning just a flicker of fervor.

"I love you, you know," he said. "I don't want to leave you. There are hospitals in Austin."

She separated them slowly, gently, her hands on his chest. "I know you do, Cash. I really do. And I love you, too. But it's not the same. I… I guess we've just been too close all these years. And all I've been thinking about all through school was getting as far away from Louisiana as I can."

She hugged him, then kissed his cheek. "I guess I just don't have time for commitments."

He looked at her for a long moment. Then he silently hefted their bags and motioned her to open the door for him.

63

❧ ❧ ❧

As they checked out, the man behind the counter gave Cassius a curious look. Cassius had tried to make small talk with the clerk, as he was prone to doing, but MaryLou thought it was just to corroborate his story of his poor parking being due to some phantom car, not his alcohol levels from the bar.

"Nope," the clerk responded. "We had no other guests check-in last night. I didn't see another car in the lot this morning either."

"I'd better drive," was all she said. "Until your coffee kicks in."

Another sheepish look.

She went straight to the driver's seat and buckled up. She was going to drive today, partly because she wanted to, partly because she was miffed at him for driving buzzed only a few hours before. As he sauntered to the car, she started it up and they got back on the highway.

The rest of the drive was pretty quiet and uneventful. They got out of the rural desolation of east Texas rather quickly, and in a matter of hours were in the hyper-urbanized center of Houston. Once through the sprawl of suburb, then city, then suburb again, they turned off I-10 northwest onto State 71 at Columbus and onto a two-lane country road through La Grange toward Austin.

Cassius's condo was central to the state-building, in between the Capitol and the University of Texas. It was tall and had floor to ceiling tinted windows all along the façade.

"Pretty fancy," she said. "And the company's paying for it?"

"Until I find a place," he said. "Maybe need a roommate for a while." He paused. "This is nothing like we're used to," he said.

"No," she responded. "Nothing anymore is going to be like what we're used to."

They unloaded his two suitcases out of the trunk and stood them on the curb. "Want to see my place?" he asked.

She shook her head. "I don't think it would be a good idea, Cash. Let's just say our goodbyes here and promise to keep in touch."

He managed a smile. "I meant what I said. Lots of hospitals here. It's the Capitol, you know…"

She grinned. "No kidding? I thought the capital was El Paso!"

He stepped and put his arms around her, aimed a kiss but she turned her cheek. She hugged him tightly. "You be a good boy," she said, stepping out of the embrace. "Lots of beautiful women down here, you know. I checked."

"Southern belles?"

She laughed. "Exactly."

"But I already have one," he pleaded, arms out.

"And you always will," she said. "Keep in touch."

"More than that," he said, something new in his eyes. "Like they say, 'Love conquers all'."

For as long as they had known each other and as much as they had been through together, they probably should have had a longer farewell, MaryLou thought as she waved at him one last time before pulling away. But she knew if she'd gone up to his condo with him, her resolve would have been sorely tested.

Of course, I'll miss him, she thought. But her excitement to start her new life on the west coast trumped any feeling of sentimentality. Cassius, unlike her life in Louisiana, was not just another bad memory in her rearview, but a happy one, rewarding instead of anguished.

But her new life lay out on the road ahead.

CHAPTER FIFTEEN

It was the steamy jungles of Panama all over again, the firing starting seconds after I jumped off the Mike boat. I and five others splashed from the river into the mud and ran for the cover of brush past a small palm-strewn beach amid a thunderstorm of fire. Our guys ahead of us were under heavy attack. Another case of bad intelligence; there seemed like a thousand more of the rebels than we were led to believe. It wasn't long before I was hearing the shouts from the rest of my platoon of fourteen men and two officers, the moans, the terrified screams as I emptied my M-16 even before we hit the edge of the jungle, then I suddenly had an M-2 Browning .50 caliber in my hands, emptying that, running, running, picking up an M203 40 mm. grenade launcher, running again, shouting, picking up weapon after weapon from the bloody and shattered carcasses of Special Forces support who had gone before us, and of fellow comrades and rebels alike.

I was shrieking once again as the explosion threw me and two other guys unconscious into the air. I awoke soaked in the usual sweat. The relief I felt every time was real—I wasn't on that stretcher with a piece of hot metal sticking out of my neck, but alone in my bed, shaking, instinctively feeling the scar just behind my carotid artery. I shuddered every time I did it, remembering the doctors shaking their heads in disbelief. A quarter-inch forward and I would have bled to death, they told me. If I had fallen off the stretcher or they dropped it or one of the medics got hit while running, the shrapnel would have dislodged and sliced the artery.

I tore off the drenched T-shirt and looked at the clock. Four-thirty in the morning.

After trying for half an hour, I decided I'd never get back to sleep and got up and warmed yesterday's coffee. I slipped on my sweat suit, flipped a slice of rye bread into the toaster and got down a jar of peanut butter. I watched the morning news as I ate: a couple of shootings in Oakland, a robbery in Sausalito, local political blo-viating, a car-jacking in the City, the threat of a drought together with the threat of mass floods this winter because of all the forest fires—the usual stuff. When it was finally daybreak, I went for a three-mile run. At home I showered, had another cup of coffee and a second piece of peanut butter toast. I put on grey slacks, an open-collared dress shirt, my shoulder holster, and carried a navy-blue blazer to the kitchen. My P.I. costume, I called it. Yes, most P.I.s don't go to work packing, but I considered it an essential piece of wardrobe. My piece of choice was a Ruger LCR .38 revolver, mostly because it was hammerless, to avoid snagging on clothing because I knew if and when I ever had to use it, it had to come out pretty damn quick. And in that regard, I also chose to fit it with a Crimson Trace Laser grip because I wouldn't have time to do a sightline. If I'd learned one thing in both my military and police service it was what the Boy Scouts have known all along: "Be Prepared!"

I made some fresh coffee and stared out the window, thinking again about the McCovey Cove girl and her torrid affair with my best friend. (To my astonishment, I had completely forgotten to ball him out about not confiding in me about her.) Mainly, I was thinking about *why* she was thrown in the water. It was certainly getting convoluted. I mean, once you kill someone, you either leave the scene pronto or take the body somewhere to dispose of it if you don't want it to be discovered. And if you don't care whether it's discovered, why not just leave it where you smoked her? And in this case, it was even more curious. If you think you've killed her and don't care if she's discovered, but don't *want* to leave her there, why go through the trouble of throwing her in the drink? Why not a garbage can, or deserted alley? And if you realize she isn't dead, why wait around until she is? I mean, why not give her the old *coup de grace*? (It always bothered me when people mispronounced it *koo-de-grah*.)

And finally, as the well-dressed doctor had said, someone going bonkers in panic can lose all sense of reason. I was becoming convinced that the perp knew she was still alive when he decided to throw her in the water, but didn't know she was dead by the time he finally did it.

And then there's the *where* of it. Where was she at the time? Was she hiding out from her husband? Whence was the poor thing launched into the bay? (Put "whence" in the same drawer as "opine.") I quickly took a mind's-eye tour of the bay. Sausalito? Tiburon? Angel Island? Emeryville? Alameda? Candlestick Point? No, I understood Ranger Kaufman's logic and she was right—it had to be very close to where McCovey Girl was found. I was sure the cops would conclude the same by calling the MM&P gang, but I made a mental note to call a bar pilot friend for his guess. Those guys all had to know the tides and currents down to the centimeter. (What's the MM&P? The union of bar pilots and licensed deck officers called the International Organization of Masters, Mates and Pilots, sometimes referred to by landlubbers like me as the "masturbating pilots.")

The Krupps buzzed and I filled my Notre Dame Class Reunion cup and sat down at the breakfast counter. The more I thought about it, the more repetitiously I was concluding that it couldn't be done—you couldn't tell by tides and currents where Point B would be if you threw an object into the bay at Point A. But I'd call my friend anyway.

Hell, who says she wasn't thrown off a boat?

CHAPTER SIXTEEN

I went outside and picked up the paper to see whether it had hit the press yet. I dropped the front World News section of the *Chronicle* on the kitchen table and thumbed through the Bay Area section for local news. On Page Five there was a one-paragraph story about a boy at Oracle Park discovering an unidentified drowned woman in McCovey Cove. No other details, other than the usual call for "anyone having information about…" and that a police investigation was "underway." Slightly relieved that no other personal details were revealed, I went right to the Sports section and checked the latest score on the Giants' depressing collapse after three World Series wins in five years. Sure enough, they were losing a series to the Dodgers, no less. Adding insult to injury.

I had barely finished my second cup when the phone rang. It was Bill Ralston. I looked at the clock as I picked up the phone.

"Wassup, Bill? Kind of early, isn't it?"

"Apparently not for the M.E.," he said. "He just called and asked me to come over."

"Did he say why?"

"Nope. Just said he wanted to show me something he'd forgot about. I thought you'd like to join me."

I looked at the clock again and pulled the toaster plug out of the wall as I spoke. "It's almost seven. Let me cram some scrambled eggs and if I can beat the traffic, I'll meet you at the morgue at eight."

"OK, I'll wait outside for you. I'll be alone."

❧ ❧ ❧

We found the doc with his feet up reading the paper and the first thing I noticed was that he was blowing smoke rings. The second thing was that he wasn't wearing his garish yellow plaid trousers, just an ill-fitting pair of jeans that only accentuated his paunch.

"I didn't think smoking was allowed in the morgue," I said casually as we entered.

He smiled. "It isn't," he said. "But I don't think cigarette smoke is going to harm anyone in here." Then he chuckled.

After a few more pleasantries he put out the cigarette, and got up and walked us into the chilly cadaver room.

"At first I thought nothing of it during the autopsy," the rotund doc said. "But something about it kept nagging at me, and I finally analyzed it."

Ralston and I looked at each other as he moved to the drawer labeled "Kowalski" and rolled out the sheet-covered body of MaryLou. He didn't uncover her top half, but lifted the sheet up from her lower torso until it uncovered her abdomen. He gently rolled her over onto her side and pointed at the tattooed heart on her cheek. Then he lowered his finger and pointed directly to a tiny word tattooed next to it: "CINDY."

Ralston and I bumped heads as we leaned down to take a closer look at the tattoo.

"Cindy?" I said, looking at Ralston. "Johnny never mentioned any Cindy to me."

"Not a nickname or anything?"

I shook my head. "No. When he told me about the heart, I just assumed she had it done in his honor." Pause. "Or whatever the word is."

The good doctor dropped the sheet on MaryLou's back. "Except for one thing," he said dramatically. "The name isn't a tattoo."

"It's not?" Ralston and I almost said it simultaneously.

The doc shook his head. "It was written there sometime after the original heart was tattooed on," he said.

"I'm guessing either right after she was killed or shortly before," I said. "Or else Johnny would have seen it and certainly mentioned it to me."

"How do you know it's not a tattoo?" Ralston asked.

"I did a scraping," he said. "It was written in indelible ink, probably some kind of special pen artists usually carry. I have a friend who does freelance diagrams in India ink for the U.S. Patent Office. It's almost the same as the chemical used in voting ballot inks, silver nitrate. It's preferred because it's soluble in water and makes an inky black solution. When put on the skin, however, silver nitrate reacts with the epidermis salt present on it to form silver chloride, stays black and which is *not* soluble in water and clings to the skin. It can't be washed off with soap and water. It can't even be scoured off, not even with hot water, alcohol, nail polish remover, or bleach. The ink will only disappear as the old skin cells die and get replaced by new ones."

"Wow," Ralston said.

"Wow is right," I echoed.

"It very much is *like* a tattoo, but it wasn't done at the same time that little red heart was, I'd bet my mortgage on it," the doc said. I fleetingly wondered where he lived.

"Think it's an autograph?" Ralston said. "A lot of criminologists and forensic people are convinced murder perps who think they've committed the perfect crime usually leave some kind of hint around to show how clever they are."

"You saying the killer's name is Cindy?"

"Could be," he said. Or it's a phony name, maybe a rhyme. Windy? Mindy? Lindy?"

My brain was really working hard as he spoke. "You know," I said, "or it could be the perp wants us to *think* somebody named Cindy did it."

CHAPTER SEVENTEEN

On the way back to our cars, Ralston and I did some more guessing about the name Dr. Feinberg found on poor MaryLou's butt, but didn't really come up with anything even close to logical. We parted ways, again agreeing to keep each other posted on developments.

"Oh, by the way," I said before he left. "I tried to interview Kowalski. He clammed up, of course, referred me to his lawyer. What did you guys find out?"

"Nothing much, he's got an alibi, although weak."

"He had a black eye."

Ralston laughed. "Yeah, we asked him about it. All he said was it none of our business."

"Same here," I said. "I wouldn't be surprised if the dead woman gave it to him."

He just shrugged. "We'll probably never know," he said and peeled off.

In my car, I called Lynch, using the number of the burner phone I insisted he buy to make and take calls from now on. Most cops trusted their pals at IA only as far as they could hurl a refrigerator, and Johnny and I agreed that there was an outstanding chance his home phone would be tapped and his registered cell phone would otherwise be compromised. He picked up even before the first buzz was finished.

"Hi, Steve. What've you got?"

"Just had another meeting with the M.E. and Ralston," I said. "Seems the M.E. found another tattoo on your girlfriend's ass, the name 'Cindy.' Ring a bell?"

"Cindy? There was no such name on her tattoo, Stevie. Just the heart."

"You sure? When was the last time you saw it?" I had to chuckle a little. "Dumb question?"

He managed a chirp himself. "C'mon, pal. Would I miss somebody else's name?"

"Answer the question."

I heard him sigh. The sigh said if you weren't my best friend I'd hang up on your ass! "I told you already, it was the night before her husband rolled up on us and took her home. I guess it was about a couple weeks before she was found. The last time we were together. We wanted to rent a small motel on Van Ness but couldn't get a room so we just had dinner on the wharf in the middle of all the tourists."

"Smart, pal. Smart. You'd never bump into anyone you knew there. And you saw no other marks on her at all?"

"No, man. Just the heart. And I don't even know anyone named Cindy."

"No co-workers? Relatives? She even *mention* the name at all? Ever?"

"Nope, never. Where are you?"

"Right outside the M.E.'s. Have you told Ralston or anyone that she'd been staying at her friend Lucy's?"

"No. I don't even know Lucy's last name."

"Well don't. Don't say a word. Want to have a drink?" And before he could answer, "Let's go to the Spinnaker in Sausalito. You buy lunch."

"Talked me into it," he said. "What time?"

"I have some calls to make but it's still early. Make it closer to one-thirty."

He buzzed off and I cranked up the car. It wasn't far to San Francisco General. I knew I wouldn't get far on the telephone, so decided to visit the personnel department in person.

The office was one of several in the business section of a large building across from the hospital. Miscellaneous posters about safety and sex harassment, lists of various government regulations, pale green walls, the usual boredom. My P.I. creds got me through the Information station, and again past an unarmed guard and a secretary, and into the tiny office of the Personnel Director, a Mrs. Barbieri. She was a middle-aged woman, I guessed fiftyish, but stylishly dressed in a dark blue pants suit and white blouse with a large floppy bow at the throat, her hair carefully coiffed, fingernails long and professionally done.

I apologized for not having an appointment, flashed my creds again, and explained that I was working on a case in which a woman by the name of Lucille came up, who worked here at SF General, but that I didn't have a last name. I acknowledged that I realized Mrs. Barbieri couldn't give out the woman's address or phone number, but that all I needed was a last name and I could go through other channels to contact her. Satisfied with that, she clasped her hands in front of her and apparently didn't need to check any files.

"Well, Mr. Lombardo," she said, "we happen to have two Lucilles working here."

"Lombardi," I corrected, and waited.

"A Lucille Reynolds, rotating in ER and Surgery, and a Lucille Mendoza in the Maintenance Department."

"That's great," I said. "You certainly seem to have a good memory."

"It's my job," she smiled. "Would you like to interview them?"

"No, no thank you," I said, standing. "A phone call is all I need. Thank you again."

She smiled again and stood. "Glad I could help."

❦ ❦ ❦

Of the two Lucilles, Reynolds in Surgery and Mendoza in Maintenance, I took a wild guess that the former would be one to start with. I also guessed that she'd be working the eleven-to-seven swing shift in ER with MaryLou Kowalski, and was probably just having her first coffee at this time of the morning. I didn't want to tip Ralston off by asking him to trace a Lucille Reynolds, R.N., so I got her unlisted number from one of my insider contacts at City Hall.

The voice that answered was indeed sleepy, but snapped to attention pretty quick.

"Ms. Reynolds?" I asked. "Lucille Reynolds?"

"Who wants to know? Who is this?"

"My name is Steve Lombardi," I said, speaking quickly. "I'm a private investigator friend of Police Inspector John Lynch who I'm sure you know your friend MaryLou Kowalski was involved with and it's very important that I speak with you in private." All that in one breath.

"My God," she said. "I don't want anything to do with this and I'm not talking to anyone about her. How did you get my number?"

"That's not important, Ms. Reynolds. But my friend John is a suspect in her murder and you might have information that could clear his name."

"Murder? Is that what they think?"

"Yes, ma'am. So far they're keeping it from hitting the papers. Please, can we meet somewhere private?"

"Private! Are you insane? I have no idea who you are!"

She had a point. I could be MaryLou's killer, for all she knew. Or someone working for the husband trying to find out where she lived. "If I give you my full name, address and ID number, will you call the Attorney General's office in Sacramento and verify that I am who I am? Er … who I say I am? Or … whatever?"

A pause. "You could have anyone's ID. I'm calling the—"

"Please!" I hastily interrupted. "Please don't, Ms. Reynolds. Look, would you call Inspector Lynch himself and ask him about me? Ask him to tell you something secret about his friend Steve Lombardi and then call me back and ask me the secret. How about that? Would that convince you?"

Silence. She was thinking hard.

"Ms. Reynolds?"

"What do you want to know?"

"I'm not sure. Maybe some things about MaryLou that even Johnny wouldn't know. Anything…"

Silence again. Then, "What's his number?"

I let out a long sigh. Thanking her for at least giving me a chance, I gave her Johnny's burner number and my own. "Wait half an hour," I said, "to give me a chance to alert him to your call."

She actually let out a laugh. "Bullshit. What do you take me for? You'll give him the secret information that I'll just bounce back to you. What would that prove?"

Smart girl. "OK, you're right. Call him immediately and call me right back. Tell him his middle name is Timothy."

I thought I heard her chuckle as she hung up quickly and I said a silent prayer that Johnny not only would answer his burner phone right away, but also that he'd believe her. Not too many people knew his middle name.

I noticed a coffee shop down the street and walked to it. I sat in a corner nursing a latte and reading the rest of the *Chronicle* that I'd missed when Ralston called. When I finished, I checked my watch and saw that a half hour had passed. Now a new set of probables flashed across my brain. She probably hadn't bothered to call Johnny and called the cops after all. Or, she probably called and he didn't answer. Or he probably answered but didn't believe her. Or he probably was too shocked by her call and hung up on her. Or he probably did actually speak with her but was reluctant to share anything personal.

Or, hell, she was now probably packing her bags and moving to Arizona.

But ... for all that, why hadn't he called me back?

My phone rang ten minutes later.

"Mr. Lombardi?"

"Steve."

"I spoke with John Lynch."

"I take it you hadn't met him before."

"MaryLou talked about him a lot, but no, she never introduced us. She always intended too, though. At least she said so."

I let out another sigh. "If I sound a little relieved, it's because you sound a lot friendlier than before."

She laughed. "Sorry. We had a long chat. He sounds like a nice guy. He's extremely upset."

"Upset! That's an understatement. Try 'scared shitless.' But I'm glad you got along. Do you want to ask me anything personal?"

She paused, then said, "Actually, I'm starting to believe you're for real, but what the hell."

"Shoot."

"When you and he were working together, you had a pickup routine you used on young women. What was it?"

My turn to laugh. "God, he could have picked anything but that."

"Don't tell me it actually worked?"

"Ms. Reynolds, John Lynch is a very handsome dude! I was just along for the ride. And yes, it worked a lot."

"So ... what was it, anyway?"

"Can you see me blushing?"

"Come on ..."

"Three options. Bar and drink, John's place and drink, her place and drink."

"Bingo," she said. "How do you want to do this?"

77

I still could hear a bit of caution in her voice and I acknowl-edged it to assuage her. "Whatever you like. How about you pick a spot? Say, a crowded coffee house or restaurant. As long as we can carry on a conversation." I paused, thinking of another carrot. "And I'd be willing to bet you'll be packing."

"I carry a taser when I'm working. Otherwise, a Beretta .22 with hollow points."

"That's illegal, of course. But having said that, you need bigger. That .22 will just piss someone off. We should talk about it. What time?"

"Let's make it a bit before lunch. There's a big Starbuck's in the Marina, on Chestnut. Tell me what you look like. If I like what I see I'll sit down."

CHAPTER EIGHTEEN

It had been over sixty hours already since MaryLou dropped off Cassius at his condo. She felt like she had done so much already. She had stopped for the night in a town east of El Paso—she slept well that night as she had the bed, and room, all to herself. She even met some folks along the road at diners and gas stations. Mostly truck drivers and, of course, some had tried to hit on her—that was par for the course. Nonetheless, she found most folks generally cordial and welcoming.

After El Paso, she had turned north toward Albuquerque. Her plan was to go through northern Arizona and see the Petrified Forest and Grand Canyon before she made it to California. The Petrified Forest was a real let down, it was one of those places where, after you've seen 100 yards of the park, you felt like you had already seen the whole thing. She had even been unaware she was in a National Park until the sign alerted her. She had thought all the petrified logs were just desert boulders or rocks she had been seeing for half her drive.

As big of a letdown as the Petrified Forest was, the Grand Canyon left her speechless. For the first time she had no witty retort. It was one of those places where once you see it, you just think: "I get it." The definition of geologic erosion in a single panoramic vista. The pure size and the way the colors danced between the ochres and purples was mesmerizing. She stayed there for hours longer than she intended. She even ran into a group of elk. They were the biggest animals she had ever seen and were a reminder that the Grand Canyon was a wildlife park, not just a massive river crater cutting through the earth. A poor sharecropper's daughter in Mooringsport could never in her most delirious fantasy conjure such an image as now before her.

Today, though, she was passing through Arizona and heading toward Yosemite, her final stop before what they called the "Bay Area." She took two days to leisurely hit Hwy US 40, back at Flagstaff, part of the legendary Route 66, through Flagstaff, Kingman and just past Barstow. She hummed the famous Bobby Troup song in her head, "Get your kicks, on Route 66..."

At the California border she passed over the Colorado River and was amazed at the stark difference in terrain, from the bright green farmland on the Arizona side to the barren sands of the Mojave Desert surrounding the remote town of Needles. She ultimately connected to California Hwy 395 and turned all the way northward, taking the two-lane blacktop through the scorching desert, past imposing Mt. Whitney on her left and Death Valley on her right, then finally climbing to the high pine country toward Mono Lake and then west along the stunning Tioga Pass Road.

And if she was impressed with the titillating variety of California geography, she was absolutely staggered by the sight of Yosemite Valley. She almost couldn't believe what she was seeing. A deeply gouged valley surrounded by solid granite cliffs soaring at ninety degrees above towering pines. A meandering river on its floor, evenly dividing the valley east to west. A gigantic half-dome sliced neatly at midpoint by a creeping glacier millions of years ago. Dozens of gushing waterfalls throughout, adorning each side of the craggy canyon.

There was no possible way she could even start to compare this astonishing spot to her birthplace.

She collected her thoughts with great difficulty and drove the short length through the valley, looking for a campsite along the Merced River, next to the famous Ahwahnee Hotel. She found one flanked on either side by the shadows of Half Dome, one of the most spectacular pieces of granite ever conceived by whatever artistic-minded spirit composes these things.

Finding a place to park for the night was scant. After circling the site a few times, she finally found a spacious spot next to a large Class B Winnebago. MaryLou sighed, envying the comfortable-looking RV.

But she had made it! She got out, stretching her legs and arching her back with a grunt. She got out, looked around, and let the crisp pine air fill her lungs, looking around. She was disappointed she had no view of the rest of the valley to the west, it being obscured by a forest of pine trees, but it was perfect nonetheless. She felt like a totally new person.

She hadn't noticed an old blue Trans Am following her through the park and now stopping several yards away.

A man got out and waved at her. "My lucky day."

"Huh?" MaryLou turned around.

"What are the odds I get the prettiest girl in Yosemite as my neighbor tonight," the man said, pointing at her.

"Oh, yeah?" she responded sarcastically. She was used to getting hit on, but this was a bit much. "Bug off, mac!" she shouted across the space. She looked around for a better spot. This guy was obviously drunk, or stoned, or something. Both? He appeared to be as disheveled as his car.

"You alone now, right? That's great, we can get to know each other."

Confused and now frightened, MaryLou turned back to her car. She started to open the door as the man approached to only feet from her.

"Hold on," he said. "We have to talk. You don't know me but I met your boyfriend a few days ago. He told me you would be ending up here. Showed me a picture of you too, but you're way prettier in person."

Her boyfriend? Who would that be?

My God! She gripped the handle of her car door in such shock her fingernails dug into her palms, as she flashed back to the B&B scene with Cassius. He had said a Trans Am was back in their motel parking lot. This was the stranger Cassius had a drink with! He was following her! But for how long? Since San Antonio? Since Las Cruces?

She couldn't stifle a frantic whimper as she yanked the door farther open and started to get in when the Winnebago door swung open behind her and a woman stepped out with a short single-barreled shotgun extended. She looked at MaryLou and then pointed the gun right at the aggressor.

"I think she's had enough of you," the woman said angrily. "Why don't you hit the road before this makes you look like a Cyclops." She shook the rifle at him.

"We was just talkin'," he responded, backing away. "I wouldn't hurt her. I came all this way to see her."

MaryLou looked back at the woman, shaking her head as hard as she could.

"No, I think you're going to get in the car and drive off now." She lowered the gun to point at his groin. "Or maybe you'd like to be a soprano..."

The man looked back at MaryLou, and complied with the order. As he drove off in an exhaust-filled haze, he said through his window, "I'll be seeing you. I know where you're going. San Francisco!"

MaryLou stood at the car door, still frozen, then started to shake.

"Welcome to California, sweetie," the woman said. She had tucked the gun behind the Winnebago door, and when MaryLou put her hands to her face and started sobbing, she put her arm around and hugged her.

"Oh, you poor thing. Scared the shit out you. Why don't you come in my RV for a while? You'll feel safer. I promise you he won't come back. Here, I'm Tiffany. Come on inside."

MaryLou suddenly did feel safe; it was over now. So she figured she might as well relax inside the RV.

Inside was even larger than she expected. She'd never been in such a vehicle and marveled at its interior. There was a futon mattress along a wall and a small table with bench seating nearby. Toward the rear was a small bedroom and a tabled seating area. The place was messy, but not dirty. As MaryLou looked around, Tiffany reached in the fridge and grabbed a couple of little Coronito beers and handed one over to MaryLou.

"So, what's your name now, dear?"

"MaryLou."

"MaryLou, where're you from? Oklahoma?" Tiffany laughed.

"Louisiana, actually."

"So, what brings you out here?"

MaryLou told her about her road trip with Cassius and about the B &B episode.

"Man, we should have got his license plate. The guy should be arrested!" Tiffany said.

MaryLou took a long sip on her beer. "I'm going to a job in San Francisco."

"You're moving here alone? With no man?"

"I left him in Austin. Well, he was never my man, but yeah, I'm making the trip solo. Stretching my wings, or flying alone, or whatever they say. Starting a whole new life."

"Flying solo. Well that's the way to do it." Tiffany began pacing around the trailer, picking up stray clothes and tossing them into the back room. "I've sworn off men for the past few years now and let me tell you, there's nothing I miss there."

MaryLou perked up at this. "Wow, you've been alone for a few years? I've been enjoying my freedom for only three days and while it's been great, I can't imagine not being with anyone else for years."

Tiffany sat back down, closer to MaryLou this time. "Who said anything about 'alone'? I just said I've not been seeing men. Come on, girl, there's still half the damn population when you remove men, aren't there?"

It clicked. MaryLou had never met a lesbian before. Well, maybe she had, but in Louisiana she was never one to ask, or even assume. She noticed at that moment how pretty Tiffany was, there was a spark in her. Tiffany wasn't young, but did not look old either. MaryLou pegged her in her early forties. She had long hair, deep brown eyes and even with no draft in the RV, her loose blouse always seemed to be flowing in a breeze.

"You don't get it, miss southern belle?" Tiffany smiled.

MaryLou realized she had been staring and her expression could be read clear as a bumper sticker on her forehead that said, *Ignorant*.

She blushed. "Sorry, just, I...I don't think I've met anyone who's...uh...'gay' before."

"I figured as much. Don't worry, I promise you it's safer in here with me than with that asshole outside."

MaryLou felt safe. She also felt high. The half of a beer she was sipping was soothing her out and she had just almost forgotten about the man in the blue Trans Am until Tiffany reminded her.

MaryLou continued, looking to change to a more casual subject so she could gain back some "cool" credibility. "How long have you been here in Yosemite?"

"On and off, about a month, actually. I go trekking and then come back to this spot. I drive around a lot, too. I came here after spending some time up north in the Lost Coast working for some cultivators."

"Lost Coast?" MaryLou had never heard of that place before, and she prided herself in the research she did about California before her move, hoping to at least sound like a local before she even arrived. This, however, was never in any book and wasn't on any map she'd seen.

"Yeah," Tiffany said. "It's this stretch of coastline north of Sonoma, where the 101 freeway veers inland for some miles through Mendocino and Humboldt counties before linking back up with the ocean near the border with Oregon. Since no highway runs through that stretch of coast, it's said to be lost in time. And let me tell you, it is."

"Wow," is all MaryLou could think to say. In just a short amount of time, Tiffany had already become the coolest person she'd ever met. Someone with a shotgun traveling back in time by herself. California really was everything she had heard of.

Tiffany reached across the table and grabbed a lighter. She pulled a hand-rolled joint from behind her ear, hidden beneath her long hair and lit it, staring right at MaryLou the entire time.

As she offered it across the table, MaryLou shivered. California was going to be a trip, whether she was ready for it or not.

MaryLou was late. The traffic heading through Merced and then up Hwy 99 didn't help, but she couldn't blame that entirely. MaryLou didn't regret staying the extra two days touring around with Tiffany among the pine trees and granite walls, hiking around Mirror Lake, visiting the many waterfalls, picnicking at Tenaya Lake. She marveled at the impossibility of such a beautiful place even existing, and simply smiled and nodded her head in humorous agreement when Tiffany had said that Yosemite Valley was where God spent His vacations.

MaryLou knew that this visit, Yosemite Valley and Tiffany, would be one of the many milestones to come in her life.

But now those two wondrous days meant she started work in two hours and still hadn't gotten to her as yet unseen new apartment.

MaryLou smiled. Sexually she was a newborn babe, only as experienced as the men she had allowed to second base, and even they were few and far between. She smiled yet again at her continual encounters with the insistent and unbelieving Cassius and his dreams of future romance and passion. But her two nights with Tiffany changed everything she knew not only about intimacy, but also about her own body. She always thought she was the one most familiar with herself, but during those two days, Tiffany seemed to know what her body wanted before she even did. She was the stranger to the relationship Tiffany was having with her body, the awkward misgivings getting in the way of the chemistry between Tiffany's touch and her skin.

Now she was having a certain level of shame and guilt as she left 99 and guided along 580, then through Oakland onto 80 North to the Richmond-San Rafael Bridge. She caught her first glimpse of San Francisco across the bay to her left. It was beautiful, even through the low fog that seemed to huddle it selfishly. Across the bridge and onto 101 South, it was overcast as she weaved through Marin County, getting closer to San Francisco. That overcast, she would learn, was what locals called a "marine layer" subject to low fog rolling in right under it unexpectedly.

MaryLou exited the tunnel in Sausalito and was greeted by a sheet of gray. The fog was so thick she had driven over the Golden Gate Bridge and was slowing through the pay-direction toll booth before she even realized what she had just missed. The city's most iconic landmark, the image of San Francisco she had been dreaming about for years. She had crossed it in a matter of minutes without even realizing she was on a bridge, let alone one as famous. But she was late and had no time to pull over and try to catch a glimpse of the orange iron or flashing lights through the misty haze.

San Francisco, and her future, awaited her. MaryLou had arrived, in more ways than one.

CHAPTER NINETEEN

I quickly dialed Johnny's burner and again he answered before the first buzz was finished.

"What'd she say?" He was almost breathless.

"I think we convinced her I was legit. She's a smart cookie. She even told me she carries."

"At SFGH, a lot of night nurses also carry tasers these days. Even some of the docs. Not like the old days, believe me. But we actually had a nice talk. She sounds as shook up as I am."

"Well, tell me about it later," I said. "I have to change our lunch to dinner. I got a better offer."

"Can't wait. Same place?"

We rung off and I checked my watch. Not enough time to zip home and spiffy up a bit, so I thought I'd go and case where she lived. When I got her phone number, my City Hall contact also got the phone company to give me her address.

It turned out she lived in a little in-law apartment attached to a large brick house on outer Greenwich, close by the Presidio and Liverpool Lil's where Johnny and I had met a few days before. I parked several doors away and walked the neighborhood a bit to get a better perspective. I figured if Lucille suddenly appeared on her way to Starbuck's I'd just keep strolling like any other passerby. After all, she didn't know what I looked like.

The apartment looked to be spacious, not cramped at all, with its own entrance next to a two-car garage with parking room beside it for a third car. The garage was closed, and as I sauntered by, I glanced through a small window and saw an empty space and a brand-new white Tesla. In the open space beside the garage was an old tan Honda Civic, circa 1995, which I guessed was Lucille's.

Since she was obviously still home, I walked back to my car and made it over to the Marina Starbuck's. Once again, the parking situation made me wish I'd used Uber, but I finally stashed the car in a half-red zone in front of a Chinese laundry three blocks away.

Inside Starbuck's was a laugh. I had to be easily twice as old as the oldest person in the place. Each table was occupied by either a group of teenagers staring at their iPhones, or a twenty-something tapping away at a laptop computer. The teenagers were grungy, long-haired and needed shaves. The twenty-somethings were snappily dressed, some even with neckties. The few adult females in the place were all dressed in black pantsuits. Their blouses were either white or red. There was a large cup of something foamy in front of everyone.

I found a window table and sat down without ordering. Since I'd finished the *Chronicle,* I fished around for something to read and the best I could do was a magazine called *Futurist.* Inside were pages and pages of diagrams, charts and computer screens, all described in a language that looked a lot like English, but was totally unintelligible to me.

To waste time, I found a crumpled *Chronicle* and attacked the crossword puzzle.

I saw her walk by on the sidewalk beyond my window, ostensibly surveying the traffic as if waiting for someone, but furtively checking out the patronage inside. At least I thought it was her. The right age bracket, attractive with blonde shoulder-length hair and a sensible purse hanging from a shoulder strap. She wore clean, tight-fitting jeans with the proper shredded holes in the front, and a red-and-white sweatshirt with "Badgers" emblazoned across the front.

I lifted my head slightly, as if seeking better light to read the crossword. Out of the corner of my eye I saw her do something like a double-take, and then she walked back to the corner, watched the traffic some more, and then turned slowly and entered the shop.

I looked up expectantly, putting down the newspaper and making sure she saw me. She met my gaze, gave me a chin-up nod in greeting and came over to my table. I stood, pulling out a chair.

"Mr. Lombardi." A statement, not a question.

"Steve," I said. "I take it I passed muster."

She sat down and put her purse over the back of the chair. "Let's just say you and Mr. Lynch must have been quite a pair," she said with a knowing smile. "Even your hair makes you look boyish."

I grinned back. "And as I said, I was always just along for the ride. Can I get you something? I've never been in a Starbuck's."

She raised her eyebrows. "Really? I once met a weird guy who said he'd never been in a McDonald's, but ... *really?*"

I just shrugged. I'd never been in a McDonald's, either, but wasn't about to admit it. You'd think with all my cop experience and beating around the state with my small band I'd at least *once* been in a Starbucks, but I guess we always thought it too chic, or whatever. Anyway, I decided not to try and explain it to her.

"You just give your order and your name to the barista and he'll call you when it's ready. I'll have a vanilla latte."

Barista? I got up, found my way to the ordering counter and ordered her latte and the same for myself.

"Size?"

"What? Oh, size. Medium," I said.

"Grande."

"Medium," I said again. Maybe he didn't hear me.

"Grande," he repeated.

"Doesn't that mean large?"

"Large is venti."

I decided he was speaking another language so I paid on the spot without asking why 'venti' meant 'large'. Whatever happened to plain English? In two minutes, another guy called my name, gave me the lattes and I went back and sat down. Pretty slick, I had to admit.

'So," I started, "do I call you Lucille, or …?"

"Lucy. My brother called me 'Lulu' until I was old enough to crack him across the mouth."

We each took a sip, still sizing each other up. My latte was kind of sweet, but not bad at all.

"Where are you from, Lucy"?

"Fond du Lac, Wisconsin. It means 'foot of the lake.'"

"I've heard of it," I said. "Didn't something famous happen there once?"

"It's where that picture was taken about ninety years ago, you know, that prohibitionist woman … Carrie Nation? Shows her chopping down a saloon door. It made all the papers at the time."

I laughed. "Ah yes, one of my old girl friends."

That made her laugh too, and I could tell she was slowly relaxing.

"What brought you out here?" I asked.

"I'd always wanted to get out of Wisconsin. When I finished nursing school in Madison, I flipped a coin. San Francisco or LA. Same as MaryLou."

"Did she flip a coin too?"

A shrug. "Not that she ever said so. She just decided San Francisco was for her."

"Makes me wonder how many nurses in California are from elsewhere originally," I said.

"I'd bet half," she said. "At least."

Finally she said, "What do you want from me?"

I sat back, folded my hands on the table. "Where shall I start?"

"At the beginning, said Alice." She flashed a broad smile that belied her attempt at a stern façade.

I grinned back. "*Touché.* How long have you known MaryLou?"

"Look," she said. "This has all been quite a shocker. Last night the cops were all over the hospital flashing pictures of her, talking to the docs and nurses."

"Did they talk to you?"

She nodded. "I didn't tell them much." Pause. "Hell, I don't *know* much."

"Do they know she'd moved in with you?"

"No. At least, I don't think so. They sounded like she was still with that airline bozo but had just gone missing."

I said, "Good. I don't want them to know that yet."

"Why not?"

"There was an incident at Johnny's apartment when she threatened to leave him for Johnny."

"He came to Mr. Lynch's apartment?"

I nodded. "And she was there. It was all pretty ugly."

Another long silence.

I said, "So how did you two meet?"

She sipped the latte, daintily wiped off some foam from her lip. "At work," she said. "I had just moved out from Wisconsin, just out of nursing school, as I said. She made me feel at home among some pretty obnoxious surgeons, and we just hit it off."

"Was she married then?"

"No, she had just moved out from Louisiana a few months before. Drove to Austin with a good friend from school days, someone she'd dated a few times in high school. He went to Tulane and she went to LSU. He got an engineer job in Austin but these days I think he's an engineer somewhere down the Peninsula. Cassius something. I've met him a few times."

"Were they romantically involved?"

"Not that way, no. He always wanted to be, she said, but she kept him at arm's length just as a friend. When she got married, I was her maid-of-honor. It was no big deal. One of those rent-a-parson shops in Tahoe. None of us were for it. Cassius told me in Tahoe he had been crying for days."

"So, he was at the wedding, too?"

"No, he crashed it. She thought about inviting him, but decided it would be a bad idea."

"He loved her that much?"

"Like crazy. She just insisted they were old friends bonded over their childhood."

"Speaking of which, did she have any siblings?"

She sipped more latte, wiped more foam. I had the sense she was relaxing in waves. "She has a brother, Ethan. She told me neither of them could stand their old man and Ethan ran away and joined the Navy the very day he turned seventeen."

"Is he still in?"

"Nah, he's discharged and stayed out here. He's now a car salesman in Santa Rosa."

"Back to Cassius," I said. "Did he ever give any indication that he was jealous of Walter Kowalski?"

She let out a derisive laugh. "Are you kidding? He hated the sonofabitch. We all did. He was so angry I thought a few times he would actually strangle Kowalski to death! The stories she would tell me ...!"

"Could you imagine him doing the same to MaryLou?"

A vigorous head shake. "Absolutely not! He adored her."

"So he just crashed the wedding. Was he drunk?"

"Maybe a little. Anyway, MaryLou couldn't stand any of the guy's friends. Real low-lifes. She put her foot down and said none of his friends could be Best Man. Or no wedding."

"What the hell did she see in this guy?"

"None of us could figure it out. We warned her and warned her not to do it, but she insisted she loved him." A pause. "Some kind of hypnotic control, I guess. I think it was more desperation to have someone in a new city. I have a feeling as brave as she was and let on to be, she was still insecure and nervous about being alone."

"Did she have any enemies that you know of? I mean, besides the abusive husband. Jealous friends of the husband? Co-workers? She was a gorgeous woman, maybe some jilted doctor hitting on her?"

Another head shake. "She did disappoint a few docs, and a male nurse I can think of. But no, not that I know of. Everyone loved her."

I leaned back, looked out the window, took a deep breath. "Lucy, I have to ask you something really serious. And please don't feel you have to defend or protect the poor girl."

I saw her tense a bit. "Shoot, Mr.... er ... Steve."

"Was MaryLou seeing anyone else that you know of, besides Johnny Lynch?"

She was sipping the remains of her latte, but put it down suddenly. She looked at me for a long time and I got the feeling she was studying me, making one last, final judgment.

She looked down and played with her empty cup, avoiding eye contact. "I suppose you'd have to ask Cindy about that."

"Cindy?" The name hit me like a ballpeen hammer between the eyes. I remembered our meeting that morning in the morgue. "Who's Cindy?"

"Her other lover. A Chinese woman. Didn't you know she was bisexual?"

Chapter Twenty

MaryLou was surrounded by silent action. As she glanced out the window around the shore, past the Jeffrey pines and across the lake she saw boats zipping along the shimmering water and squirrels scrambling up and across tree branches, but neither made a sound. Her mind was overwhelmed with thoughts of her unknown future and her forgettable past, leaving no more space for trivial items like the present.

Although there was still some residual snow on the ground in late March, today Lake Tahoe was blessed with sunny skies and the first warm rays of the year, bringing everyone out to bask in the much-missed balmy weather. It's not every bride who can get married in the snow wearing a short-sleeved dress and sandals—MaryLou had always been unique that way.

Just across the California/Nevada state line, in Incline Village, Nevada, MaryLou was adjusting her veil for the umpteenth time praying she wouldn't slip as she marched down the winding path to the tiny chapel. She'd been assured the ice was removed and ground salted but you could never be too careful, especially with some of Walter's friends in attendance. MaryLou's husband—well, almost-husband—her fiancé, was Walter Kowalski, a San Francisco State University dropout and current airline mechanic. He was tall and handsome, with hair a color she would laughingly call "Polish red," not quite as "Irish red" as hers, but closer to a dark auburn, approaching black. They had met when she was bringing in her old Camaro to a mechanic shop a friend at work had recommended, just south of San Francisco on the Peninsula. He, a charming and persuasive talker, had convinced her to save her money and let him fix her leaky radiator. It wasn't love at first sight, but today, after the proverbial whirlwind courtship, it felt close enough.

Their courtship was brief but intense. They had hardly dated a few months before Walter began broaching the subject of marriage. MaryLou never was one to give up her independence, but in a new city, it felt good knowing someone who had family and ties to the Bay Area. That sense of belonging and acceptance by locals was enough of a reason to put down roots with Walter. They became engaged during a trip to Big Sur. Although the proposal was expected, the manner was surprising.

Walter had driven MaryLou up a long twisting road along the Pacific Coast Highway, which stretched hundreds of miles along the Pacific Ocean, running from town to city, alternating between raw nature and cozy beach communities. This part of the road through Big Sur, just south of Monterey Bay, was famous for its panoramic vistas that seemed to change every few yards, turning the entire drive into an art gallery rather than a simple coastal roadway.

MaryLou was looking out the window into the fog, trying to peer through the gray mist to catch a glimpse of the ocean. The higher they drove up the cliffs, the less foggy it became until suddenly they emerged from the gray abyss altogether. In these parts of Northern California, the fog creates two distinct spaces, as dichotomous as a water line separating clear blue skies from the shrouded marine layers.

Walter pulled over and the two of them walked to the edge of a designated scenic outlook and stared out at the sheet of grey stretched below them, the fog becoming an ocean in and of itself, extending out to the horizon. It was sunny up here, as if arriving at Mt. Olympus where the weather is always beautiful. MaryLou was speechless, and when she turned around and saw Walter on his knee and holding up a beautiful diamond ring, she couldn't catch her breath to answer. Her nervousness made her pause, and in her pause, a reactionary smile crossed her lips. Walter interpreted her reaction as an acceptance of marriage and now here she stood, in

Tahoe about to be married, convincing herself it was still the right thing to do.

The engagement was just as brief as their courtship. MaryLou did not have many friends outside of work, but didn't wish to bring co-workers to Tahoe for a wedding ceremony. She was only there herself due to the bride's obligation to be present at her own wedding. Off-handedly she asked her fellow nurse, Lucy, to be her maid-of-honor. She also didn't want any of her family or friends from back home to attend, except her brother Ethan, but he was deployed in the Indian Ocean and couldn't get off leave in time for the ceremony.

MaryLou felt guilty not inviting Cassius to her wedding, but the truth was after she dropped him off in Texas, they had not kept in touch all that much. She was eager to start her new life in California and in so doing, had to let her past life go to some extent, even at the expense of those she used to know. Honestly, the road trip from Texas to California was so impactful on herself she felt like a new person by the time she reached the Bay Area and had changed so much she was not even the same person Cassius had left just a few days prior. In fact, she was still coming to grips with the realization that she was bisexual.

"We're ready for you."

MaryLou glanced up in the mirror and saw her assistant turning to leave.

Ready or not, her wedding was about to begin.

Everyone was already standing when MaryLou turned to go down the aisle. She kept her focus on the ground, staring straight down, muttering to herself on each step praying she got down the aisle without a stumble.

"They did a pretty good job getting most of the ice scraped off," she thought to herself as she got to the stage and turned to face her partner.

Walter was tall, his frame wide enough to surround her entirely. He smiled at her, then glanced around to the audience. MaryLou only invited a few nursing friends at the last minute upon his request. This left the audience small and intimate—only several rows, although despite her admonishments Walter had a best friend standing beside him and a few co-workers from the airport off to the side.

MaryLou glanced around, seeing some familiar faces and the unwelcome new ones. But then, in the far back she saw one very familiar face. Next to the doorway, sipping on a tall beer, was Cassius. MaryLou stood there, gazing at him. He nodded to her, lifting the beer as a toast. She nodded back in shocked robotic acknowledgment, starring at him the entire time as he drifted off behind the hors d'oeuvre tables. She turned back to Walter when the minister began speaking.

Of all days and of all people, she thought. How did he even know where we were?

No time to ponder the answer as the minister began his carefully rehearsed routine and in less than ten minutes, Walter and MaryLou were kissing as newlyweds to the applause of their guests. MaryLou was beaming, but once their embrace was over and Walter stepped down to the congratulations of his family and friends, MaryLou made a beeline to find Cassius.

He was meandering outside next to a pine tree, kicking a pine cone and polishing off a Sierra Nevada beer. MaryLou walked over to him, her dress dragging behind in the dirt and pine needles.

"Well congratulations, I guess." Cassius said as she approached.

"Thanks, what the hell are you doing here?"

"Good to see you too," he said evenly. "Ethan wrote me about the wedding and I figured my invitation must have gotten lost in the mail, and my phone number must have been lost, and my email address lost, and—"

"OK. I get it," MaryLou cut him off. "I'm sorry. It wasn't personal but we wanted a small thing, and it was short notice. Only people from the Bay Area were invited to attend."

"I always thought Silicon Valley was part of the Bay Area. And it certainly was personal. I thought we were closer than that. So suddenly I have to hear about your wedding from your brother five thousand miles away?"

"I'm sorry, it's just I feel like I'm trying to live this new life, and it's hard to hold on to the past when doing that, you know?"

"No, I don't know. Hard, or you just don't want to be my friend anymore?"

MaryLou had no answer. Well, she did, but not one she wanted to share.

Cassius continued, "So who even *is* this guy? You can't have known him very long."

"No, not that long. His name is Walter, he's a mechanic right now for American Airlines. And look, I'm sorry you feel that way but you can't show up here unannounced."

"So, you're kicking me out? After I came all the way up here? Just like that?"

"I didn't ask you to come. Please, I have to go, we can talk about this later. Maybe I'll see you soon? But announced this time."

MaryLou glanced back toward the chapel. Walter had poked his head out looking around for her. Once he saw her, he did a double-take—confused she had run away from the altar to speak to a man he had never met.

"My husband is coming," saying the word husband was foreign for MaryLou, yet the term just came to her vocabulary so naturally it shocked even herself to hear it out of her own mouth. "I'm not sure he's happy seeing me talking to you right now."

She tried to feign playful laughter; it didn't land.

Cassius looked at her and said coldly, "Fine, I'll get going."

He began to part, but looked back at her, "Yes, I'd like to see you again. But it may be sooner than you think."

MaryLou sighed and turned, nearly smashing her face into Walter's puffed-out chest.

"Who was that?" he questioned.

"No one, just an old friend."

"Did you invite him to the ceremony?"

"Nope, I think he was just here by coincidence."

"It didn't look like a coincidence. What's he doing in a tux?"

"He was at a party or something, I don't know. He's just some-body that I knew in high school," MaryLou said. She began to walk back up the chapel, hoping Walter would follow her and they could get on without a fight. She heard his footsteps crunching the pine needles behind her, but the footsteps were going in the wrong direction.

Chapter Twenty-One

It must have been the ballpeen hammer between the eyes that caused the dizziness as I walked to my car. *Bisexual?* And Johnny didn't know it? Of all the impossible things I could think of, this had to be the top. Giants and Dodgers fans hugging and kissing? Maybe. An Irishman drinking Bushmills whisky? Why not. A MAC user switching to a PC? Could be. A Ford lover buying a Chevy? If the price were right...

Johnny Lynch not knowing his gorgeous lover was also sleeping with a *woman?* Are you out of your bleeping mind?

I couldn't get it out of *my* bleeping mind as I drove home to clean up and change for our dinner.

The Spinnaker restaurant in Sausalito was built in 1960 by a local developer and a California State senator on a spit of land once referred to as Shell Beach, primarily because it was a huge mound of shells deposited not only by other local eating establishments, but also probably by a tribe of Coast Miwok who lived here before any white men arrived.

We each had a scotch at the bar while a few waiters set up one of the coveted two tables in the far corners of the restaurant, which jutted out into the bay. John could no longer flash his star and palm a twenty-dollar bill into a Maître d's hand to get the exact table he wanted in any San Francisco joint in town, but my P.I. badge and ID did the trick. Besides John still *looked* like a cop.

At a corner table one could face the bay with the rest of the restaurant patrons behind him, and wave at sailboats passing not ten yards below. It offered a breathtaking view of the City, Tiburon, ritzy Belvedere, Alcatraz, Angel Island and virtually the entire Bay Area, while imagining it was the diner's own private domain. I always considered it one of the best-kept secrets in Marin County, and on one tipsy evening a few years ago I had actually polled about two dozen diners and found that only one couple lived in Marin. They were all from France, Japan, LA, Florida ... and, well, you know what I mean.

After we sat down, we had a few more scotches, not caring whether the waiter wanted to turn the table at least three times before the dinner crowd began to dwindle.

I could tell John was anxious. When I said, "Think the Giants will take another forty years to get to the Series?" guess what he said.

"Cut to the chase, pal. What did the roommate say?" I knew he was guessing that drunken tongues speak sober truths.

"Actually, not very much," I said. "The cops had questioned everyone at the hospital of course, but she didn't tell them much about MaryLou. Claims she really didn't *know* too much, anyway."

"They had to be pretty good friends if she let MaryLou move in with her."

"Yeah, they weren't exactly strangers. They worked pretty closely at the hospital. Lucy knows all about her family and bigot father and all that, but she didn't really *know* her. You know what I mean?"

"No, I don't know, Steve. What *do* you mean?"

John had totally lost his sense of humor. I momentarily felt a little sad for him, but I understood the desperate urgency that had taken over his disposition. I had been called up before the IA guys myself several years ago, for unloading my gun at a creep and hitting him with every single shot. He looked like Clyde Barrow after Officer Hamer was through with him. But I was cleared pretty quickly when they were convinced that I was up against a fully-loaded H&K MP5.

"How well did you really know this girl, John?"

"*Know* her? Are you kidding?"

"I mean, yeah, you were sleeping together and madly in love for a year and all that. But what did you *really* know about her? Her background, her upbringing, her … er … habits?"

"Habits? You mean did I ever see her pick her nose? Or hear her fart?"

We both had to laugh. "Something like that," I said. "Like, what was she doing when she wasn't with you or working?"

John shrugged. "I don't know. Out with girlfriends, at the movies, whatever they do. Don't forget I was working, too. And she was married to that loser. We couldn't exactly see each other whenever we felt like it. I had to wait for her to call before we could arrange to get together."

The waiter came for the fifth or sixth time and we finally ordered some food and a bottle of decent wine. John knew I drank some four-dollar Chardonnay swill at home, so he treated me to a thirty-dollar bottle of Bogle Reserve.

"I hope you're on salary during your suspension," I said, toasting him.

"Death to our enemies," he said as we clinked.

"Tell me," I said. "Did she ever mention her sex life at home?"

He shook his head. "Never. Refused to talk about it and it pissed me off. None of my business, she always said. Bugged the shit out of me."

"But she was right, no?"

"Yeah, I know. I just couldn't stand the thought of her with that jerk." He threw down his wine in three gulps and filled the glass from the chilled bottle in the ice bucket.

I leaned forward a little, set my glass down, and looked at him. "John, we've been friends—Christ, like *brothers!*—for what, fifteen, twenty years?"

He nodded, serious. Took a drink. "A long time, yeah."

"So you have to level with me. No secrets, right? I'm trying to save your ass, after all."

"Yeah, so?"

"So how was your sex life with MaryLou?"

He looked relieved, sat back. "Is that all? It was great, Stevie. Like I told you, the best ever. I was going to *marry* the woman! The goddam M-word, for chrissakes!"

"Did she have any … ah, *compunctions* about it?"

He jerked his head to the side, twisted his mouth into a contortion. "Compunctions? About getting married?"

"Johnny. My man. I mean about, you know … all the sex."

"Hell no. You name it, we did it. There was nothing she wouldn't try."

"John, you and I have been through a lot. Would she—?"

Now his hands were flat on the table leaning in toward me as he cut me off. "Steve. Yes, she would. I said it and I mean it—you name it, we did it. It was like we were writing *The Joy of Sex* all over again."

"Well …"

"You're driving at something, Stevie. What's going on?"

"Over the years, we've seen some pretty bizarre … well, it *is* San Francisco after all. You know …" This was tough, as I frantically searched for the right words. But none came.

"Spit it out, pal!"

I looked at him grimly. Shoved my chair back—I guess defensively—and put my own hands flat on the table, matching his.

"MaryLou Kowalski was bisexual, Johnny. She had a female lover."

Silence. An empty, flat stare, expressionless. I'd seen it a hundred times, in interrogation rooms, at the end of a gun sight, in movies—Clint Eastwood, Vincent Price, any Tarantino movie. A combination of disbelief, disgust, betrayal, condemnation. Boring into me like a bullet, like a torturing drill, like a medieval sword.

"John?"

Stare.

"John," I repeated. "Lucy said she knew about the other woman. Her name was Cindy. The new name on the tattoo."

"And you believe this bitch nobody knows?"

"Hey, come on now, get it together. I'm just telling you what she told me."

He stood up, his face flushed with anger, and threw his glass into the ice bucket, making a clangy broken-glass noise. I'd seen him riled up, but never once seen him lose control of himself his fast.

Heads turned. Surrounding tables grew silent. The waiter at the other corner started rushing toward us.

"Sir, is there something wrong with the wine?"

I stood up myself, took a step toward him and reached out to calm him down. But before I could he lashed out a lightning fast left hook and caught me square on the jaw. I staggered back as the room started to spin, lunging sideways onto the table of an Indian family with three kids. As I reached out my hands and twirled to maintain balance, I knocked off the father's turban, which fell into a large soup tureen.

People screamed, the waiter hollered, dishes and silverware crashed about.

Sheer instinct kept me upright and I reflexively jabbed Johnny on the chin and followed with a right to his cheek. It only glanced off as he ducked and he whacked me again with a right. I was working completely on automatic as I stiffened my left palm and briefly targeted his Adam's apple. But I held back—this was my *friend*! I had never pulled a punch in my life—my philosophy had always been: *do everything you can to avoid a fight, but if you can't you damn well better win it!* I guess I was subconsciously applying that theorem when Johnny got me again with a solid left.

That did the job.

As my vision narrowed through a diminishing dark tunnel the last thing I saw was Johnny Lynch dashing through the restaurant toward the exit hallway.

Everything went black.

I awoke flat on my back looking up at a circle of dark blue Sausalito PD uniforms and two paramedics. One of them was shining a flashlight into my eyes, the way doctors do.

"He's coming around," one of them said.

I blinked my eyes a few times, then felt my aching cheek. "Where am I?"

Corny yeah, like in the movies, but I didn't recognize the ceiling. It looked vaguely like the ones I've seen a hundred times at Marin General Hospital. I kept rubbing my cheek and with the other hand reached out, if as if asking for help to sit up.

One of the paramedics took my hand and helped me. I scooched a bit to the side until I found a wall to support my back.

"You're at the Spinnaker restaurant, sir," one of the cops said. "You were apparently attacked by your dinner guest, according to witnesses."

"I wasn't attacked. We had an altercation."

"We need an ID," one of the cops said, producing a note pad. "Who was he?"

I shook my head. "No," I said. "It doesn't matter. My friend and I just had a serious disagreement."

One of the paramedics helped me up the rest of the way and I stood with my hands on my hips. I looked around and saw that a few of the nearby tables were now empty, and the Indian family had moved their meal to the other side of the room. The father had retrieved his turban from the soup tureen but hadn't put it back on his head.

"You seem to be okay, sir," one of the paramedics said. "But we'll escort you to the ER for further tests, if you'd like."

"No, no thanks," I said. "I'll be fine."

He shrugged and both of them packed up. They wrote a few notes about my "refusing" a ride to the ER, and they left.

"Sir," the note pad cop said, "your assailant also punched the Maître d' in the lobby as he ran away. We need a positive ID."

Assailant? I shook my head. "He didn't 'assail' me, officer. He's a friend of mine and we just had a fight and took a swing at each other. I'm sorry if we frightened anyone."

By now the Maître d' had approached and he was also rubbing the side of his cheek. I reached out my hand for a shake and he took it.

"I'm awfully sorry," I said. "My friend is something of a hothead. I'll pay the tab and for any damage. Are you okay?"

He nodded and actually smiled. "It's happened a few times before, when I was a waiter," he said. "Guys trying to duck the bill."

I nodded back. "I'm not pressing charges," I said, looking at the cops and then back at him. "I hope you won't either."

He shrugged. "It happens."

I looked at the cops. "So. Are we cool?"

They looked at each other. One of them said, "We'll nevertheless have to submit a 'suspicious occurrence' report."

"Do what you have to do," I said. "I'm just not IDing my friend."

"Have a nice day, sir," one of the cops said.

"What's left of it, anyway," the other one said, smiling.

"Thank you both," I said, and looked at the Maître d'.

"Mind if I finish my wine?"

CHAPTER TWENTY-TWO

My drive home was short, but by no means sweet. My cheek-bone was still throbbing, and I had a shooting pain up my shoulder and upper arm, the latter of which I didn't mention to the paramedics. They surely would have insisted on an x-ray and hustled me to Marin General Hospital, against my will, lest they be held negligent and I sued them for a jillion dollars after my arm had to be amputated. Nevertheless, I figured I probably hit the corner of a table or something on my way down, but I could stand the pain with the help of my friend Dr. Tylenol. And if it didn't go away in a few days I'd go see another doc.

The first thing I did when I got home was call John, but both his home phone and his burner didn't pick up. On his burner message I said, "Now that we have that out of our system, you still owe me a dinner." Then I took a one-armed shower, changed clothes and made myself a baloney sandwich, which, with a can of beer and my doctor friend, I took to my back deck and sat down to think as I sipped.

John had always had a short fuse. Once, when we thought we had successfully picked up a couple of real lookers at a crowded club in North Beach, it turned out they both had male escorts who didn't appreciate the hustle. I had almost talked our way out of a real skirmish when John suddenly took offense at the term "fuckin' mick" and threw a punch at one of the girls' dates. It took every waiter in the joint and a couple of patrol uniforms to break up the brawl. When the uniforms discovered we were plainclothes cops, we didn't have much trouble convincing them not to report the incident.

And I could go on and on. The time at a pool hall in the Sunset, at a Washington Square Bar & Grill (which we all called "the Washbag") softball game, even one time at a fellow cop's wedding at Grace Cathedral, for chrissakes! The guy, my lovable adorable old buddy, was a walking time bomb. A stick of dynamite with an impossibly short fuse.

So when I thought about it—the stress he was under, the IA investigation, worrisome potential damage to his career and all—I could easily understand a knee-jerk reaction. No problem, Johnny. Of course I forgive you. Let's go have that lost dinner. I hoped he could discern the feeling when he got my message.

I made a sling for my arm out of an old towel and started to pace around my deck. What were we looking at here? I could call Ralston to check in on any progress, but it would be a one-sided conversation. I'd tell him what I knew but he wouldn't share what he knew. And I understood that. When it was all said and done, he was a cop investigating a murder and I was a civilian just trying to help an old friend.

Then there were some unanswered questions: I still hadn't interviewed the kid, Cassius somebody, who was madly in love with MaryLou, nor had I spoken with her father or her brother. The husband had lawyered up, so he was a dead end. And I had to figure out who this Cindy was and how to find her.

That triggered a decision to call Ralston anyway, if only to bug him about whether he'd found any lesbian named Cindy, much less who else he'd spoken to.

I called him, got a message line, left one, and when he called me back twenty minutes later, we decided it best not to talk on the phone and to meet at John's Grill on Ellis St. just two blocks off Union Square for a late nightcap. Although it's been open for more than a hundred years—ever since the 1906 earthquake— John's local fame is as one of Dashiell Hammett's favorite hangouts, which he made famous in his mystery novel *The Maltese Falcon,* and which was where Humphrey Bogart as Sam Spade went for dinner in the movie's last scene after he finally got hold of the famously jewel-packed black bird that turned out to be stuffed with absolutely nothing.

My second trip across the bridge was much prettier since the early morning fog had long ago lifted. Because parking in downtown San Francisco these days was practically nonexistent, I parked in the Presidio and took an Uber to John's Grill. Ralston was already at the bar with Harvey Keene and I sidled up to them.

"Lieutenant, how's it going?"

He shrugged. "Slowly," he said. "Not too much info floating around. You?"

I shrugged back.

Ralston then got a good look at my face. "What the hell happened to you?"

Keene whistled. "You look like Jake LaMotta," he said.

I touched my cheek. "Johnny didn't like the idea of the Cindy tattoo," I said. "Said he never saw it, and when I suggested his girlfriend was seeing another *woman,* he slugged me."

"Jesus!" was all Ralston could say. "It looks fresh."

"Try an hour or so yeah," I said.

"Damn, we could've rescheduled," Ralston replied. I could tell he was being sympathetic to an old man who, probably, did not look well enough to be in public.

"My buddy's in bad shape, I need to keep working. I'll be alright," I tried to smile through the pain, but could feel my cheeks tremble a bit.

"Ok," he said unconvinced. "I'm afraid to ask what else you've come up with."

"Nothing. I tried to talk to her husband, but he slammed the door in my face."

"It looks like it," Keene said with a smirk.

I ignored it. "But you said he's got an alibi?"

Ralston nodded. "Yeah, he said he had to work late at the airline hangar and then stayed out 'til dawn at an all-night poker game. We're checking that story out," Ralston said. "We got to him before the lawyer did."

"Did you ever find out who 'Cindy' is?"

"Steve, you know I couldn't tell you if I did, but just between us, no. Nothing. You?"

That was quick. I knew what I came to find out even before our drinks appeared. I shook my head. "Nothing, also. I guess you've checked every tattoo parlor in town, huh?"

He just looked at me and smiled. Dumb question.

"What about the father?" I asked. "Johnny told me he was a real redneck. Maybe he knew about the Cindy thing and overreacted?"

Ralston shook his head again. "First of all, nobody seems to know anything about this alleged 'Cindy' except you and me. And second, the father has disappeared. We got the local sheriff to check on him and they can't find him. No phone, nobody home. They got a search warrant, but nothing. He's just gone."

"Interesting," I said.

But *"More than interesting!"* was what I really thought.

CHAPTER TWENTY-THREE

It was the type of day that proved Mark Twain wrong—his famous misattributed quote recalling "the coldest winter I ever spent was a summer in San Francisco," a favorite among locals gawking at shivering tourists. Today, Alcatraz wasn't an impressionist's representation through a foggy filter, but a clear, sharp island haunting the bay. It was a day that postcard photographers dream about.

I opened my blinds that morning and blinked at the sunlight. After the day I had yesterday and with the lingering shiner John left for me, I was looking forward to one of those kinds of days Twain quipped about. But that's not what was in store for me today. I don't know if it was the sharp hook my friend deposited to my cheek that shook something loose, but I knew I was forgetting some key facts to this case, and I had better jog my memory quick. It was nice meeting with Ralston but he didn't seem any further along than I was.

Since it was the perfect day for a drive, and I knew I think better when alone, I went down to my garage, fired up my old Mustang and eased out of the driveway. I know taking a drive just for fun is not something the kids want you to do nowadays with the whole climate thing, but I think they would agree this was for a good cause.

Before I knew it, I was racing south along highway 101 toward the Muir Woods and Stinson Beach exit. I turned right onto the coast highway and raced up the steep hills of Mt. Tamalpais in search of clarity, and a view.

Once you leave the east side of Marin County and head over the peak into West Marin, it becomes a whole new topography. Big

Sur minus the brand name. Gone are the suburban strip malls and high-priced local yogurt shops. Insert the wild country as it once was—redwood trees stretching as far as they are tall, deep valleys gashing the hillsides. Horses, cows, and sheep grazing behind axe-hewn fences. The occasional clapboard church on a distant knoll. Small villages with no stoplights and post offices inside the barber shops.

And tourists, always the tourists.

I swerved in and out of a few hairpin turns heading no place in particular besides the vast Pacific that lay below.

"Okay Lombardi," I thought to myself, "start thinking." There's this dead woman your best friend was dating, he's a suspect and asked your help, and you're no closer today than a week ago.

Let's review the simple facts. First: MaryLou was a nurse in SF, was married and managing two affairs. Second: She was killed with a sharp instrument to the ear canal and dumped in the bay.

That cause of death was still prickling me. How did just anyone kill a woman with a sharp blow into the ear? And what kind of tool fits that description? It can't be a coincidence that this cause of death and her profession weren't related.

"It's time I visit the hospital," I said aloud. If anything, at least I can get my shoulder looked at.

I was all the way north of Bolinas by now, so it took a while to drive back from West Marin. When I got back to Mill Valley and was about to hit the 101 toward the bridge, I stopped and called Lynch again.

But again, no answer. I made up my mind that he had Caller ID, saw it was me on the line, and simply refused to pick up. I also made up my mind that I would drive to his apartment after my hospital visit and break down the door, if I had to.

I crossed the bridge, marveled again at seeing the Farallon Islands on the horizon, this time to my right. The city was its usual mess, and I made lousy time getting across town fighting commuters to SF General, looking for parking, and finally walking into the Reception area. But I was hoping the payoff would be worth it.

I walked up to the front counter and asked to see a doctor.

"What's the issue?" A large woman behind the counter asked, not looking up. I figured since I wasn't bleeding or screaming, she could take her time.

I noisily cleared my throat and when she looked up, I pointed at my face, which I knew probably looked like a Hawaiian sunset by now. "But you should see the other guy," I said, forcing a smile.

She didn't get it. She simply nodded and printed out a form for me to fill out. Life, death, insurance, and unnecessary medical admission forms.

"It doesn't look like an emergency but I'll get a triage nurse to see you right away," she said. "Fill this out, please."

I was impressed with how fast I was able to get into a treatment room. It normally takes me mentioning my occupation to get this fast treatment. But since I'm never one to complain about good service I gleefully followed an overweight triage nurse into room C3, a surprisingly spacious room about twenty by twenty, with typical apparatus we've all seen displayed about. An examining table, covered with that butcher paper that crinkled a lot; a long stainless steel table with instruments laid out on white cloths; half a dozen sterile packs; a few chairs; an unlit lightbox to read x-rays; a scale; a mercury column and cuff to take blood pressures; a five-wheeled stool for a doc to scuffle around on the linoleum floor. A high but small window looked up at a blue sky with the first wisps of fog drifting in.

She took a serious look at me, felt my jaw, had me open and close my mouth, then made a few notes on her pad. "I'm betting I don't have to strip to my shorts," I said.

"Nope," she said, returning my smile. "And I won't even take your temperature." She left me alone.

A few minutes later, a woman who looked like a high school cheerleader burst through the door, her head buried in the clipboard she was holding. She had a blonde ponytail, barely a hint of lipstick, carefully applied eye makeup and eyes that would make Paul Newman jealous. Her lab coat hid her figure, but her legs told me all I needed to know.

She closed the door abruptly, sat down on the stool and scooted over to me, looking up at my face. "How did that happen?" she said matter-of-factly.

"I had a difference of opinion with a friend of mine," I said.

"Some friend." She reached for one of those eye gadgets they use to look into your eyeballs. I think they're called an ophthalmoscope. After checking both eyes, and feeling my jaw, she said, "Nothing broken, but I'd like to see an x-ray, just to be careful."

"Actually, I'm fine doc. It feels good, just sore, and I'm sure nothing's cracked. Nothing a couple of drinks and applying a thick steak can't fix."

She frowned. "If I put a steak on that I'd lose my license. So why are you here?"

"I'm a P.I. and came here looking into the death of a nurse who worked here. I was hoping I might be able to ask you a few questions."

"Fine by me. But your face ..."

I waved her off. "About the nurse ..."

"MaryLou." She looked visibly depressed as the name left her mouth.

"I take it you knew her?"

"Slightly. We worked together when I first started here a few months ago. We were on different floors and shifts later, but still worked with some of the same doctors. She was really efficient and it's ... it's just ..." She trailed off.

"Awful." I completed her thought.

She nodded.

"I'm sorry if this is difficult to speak about."

"It's OK. Anything to help out."

"I was curious about her cause of death."

"Drowning?" she asked.

"No, it turns out she was killed before she went into the drin—
er…bay." I caught myself.

"OH!"

"Yes, the coroner said she was killed with a long, narrow instrument jammed through her ear canal. Not something I hear or see
every day, even among homicides. I was wondering if you had any
idea of a medical instrument that fits the bill."

"You think a doctor murdered MaryLou?" she asked.

"Not necessarily, it's just something that's unusual and maybe
you know of anything that makes sense?"

"There are a lot of thin medical tools, especially in surgery. A
trocar would be one of them."

"Trocar?"

She nodded. "T-r-o-c-a-r. It's a pencil– or pen-shaped instrument with a sharp point at one end. Typically used in laparoscopic
surgery."

I scribbled in my notebook.

"Or a fine aspiration needle," she said. "It's really thin, used in
biopsies, and taking small samples from masses in the body. There
are lots of thin instruments."

I wrote "aspiration needle" in my notebook and closed it, looked
up at her. "I think that's all I need to know," I said.

"But shoving it through the auditory canal wouldn't necessarily
kill her, you know."

"Oh? The M.E. said that was the cause," I said.

She shrugged. "Well, it could be, yes. Entering the brain would
cause hemorrhage, and she'd die soon. But it would have to have
been an upward thrust, not just straight in. It would penetrate what
we call the Foramen of Monro."

"Hmmm," I said, "I'll have to check back with the M.E. Sounds
like whoever killed her knew something about the brain."

She nodded. "Do you think a surgeon killed her?" She still
looked incredulous, but seemed genuinely interested in the case.

I just shrugged. "We have nothing to go on yet. But I'm sure she
knew a lot of surgeons," I said. "I mean, working in the OR and all."

"Oh, all of them," she said.

"Any of them stand out? Was she overly friendly with any of them?"

"Do you mean dating? Oh, I don't know, we weren't that close that she'd confide in me."

"I suppose she got hit on a lot." I smiled, bowed slightly in deference. "I'd guess a lot of you do."

She got it and returned my smile. "I did hear on the grapevine once that she dated Dr. Ryan a few times."

I opened my notebook again. "Dr. Ryan?"

"Yes, but he was suspended a few weeks ago."

"Suspended?"

"Fired, actually."

"Oh, and why was that?"

"I probably shouldn't say. Besides, I've only heard rumors."

I smiled. "Rumors are my favorite."

She shook her head, but only slightly.

I gave her my best smile. "C'mon. Give me a juicy one."

She looked up and out the high window as she spoke. "They say he was dealing drugs on the side."

CHAPTER TWENTY-FOUR

MaryLou hadn't been outside of the city as often as she thought she would. Having driven through the Marin Headlands when she first arrived, and seeing the Golden Gate Bridge and bay from the viewpoint of one of the abandoned cannon placements welcoming her to her new life, she promised herself she would make it out at least once a month to the gorgeous nature that dominates Northern California. But so far, she'd only made it to Sausalito now and then, where she and girlfriends would take in the tourist-packed shops and galleries, sometimes sipping fizzy drinks in the Bar With No Name or the ritzy Spinnaker Restaurant on the point. It was a charming town, with houses dotting steep green hills above the bay, reminding one of views of the French Riviera along the Mediterranean. Or sometimes they'd take the ferry to Tiburon, another cozy one-street tourist village across the bay, again visit shops and galleries, maybe drinks and salads on the deck at Sam's, where seagulls roamed the rails, ready to swiftly steal French fries from the plates of distracted diners.

But having lived here for going on four years, she found herself more often only enjoying the trees in Golden Gate Park or the oak trees between her work and home in the south bay, or museums, or drinks at one of the trendy bars on Union Street.

"I'm still a country girl," she thought to herself now as she drove up north, seeing the full sky above her rather than in patches between concrete. She could finally breathe again.

MaryLou was excited to be leaving the urban sprawl. She was heading up to Santa Rosa, one of the bigger cities north of San

Francisco, some fifty or so miles up the coast. Her brother, Ethan, was out of the Navy and settled just an hour's drive from her. Although he wasn't able to make it to her wedding, she knew they were still as close as they were as kids, phoning or face-timing now and then. She looked forward to spending more time with him in person.

Ethan lived a few miles outside of downtown, in the heart of wine country where, instead of the brand names of vineyards you see on restaurant menus and never can afford, you see the labels of wine you buy in the grocery store because it is on sale and already is cheaper than fifteen bucks. His long driveway was an unmarked dirt break in a worn picket fence. After every curve she kept expecting to see the house, only to be met with more tall grass and dead oak trees. She finally arrived at the house, or maybe it was a barn, according to its shape. Either way, it was still leagues nicer than the shack they grew up in.

MaryLou stepped out of the car and looked around the property. As she was getting her bearings, she felt eyes watching her. She swiveled and burst into a wide smile she hadn't sported very often these days.

"Ahoy!" she called out.

"Hey there, Sis," Ethan responded.

"Permission to come aboard?"

"I'm not in the service anymore," he replied, exasperated by the running nautical jokes she had been using for years in her letters. "You can drop the jargon finally."

"Never. You may be able to take the dog out of the salt, but you can't take the salt out of the dog." She wrinkled her brow. "Or whatever they say."

"What the hell does that mean? Never heard it before. Just give me a hug. I'll show you around."

They walked around the property and reminisced about the good times, albeit it was rare, when they were kids. Ethan told her about some of his escapades in the Navy, some of the exotic places he'd visited but which she had only seen in magazines. He told her about finding a job and then being lucky enough to find this little farm that he could afford to rent in return for fixing up various equipment.

It was hot at Ethan's house, much hotter than it ever gets in the City. No fog, breeze, or marine layer to moderate the temperatures in summer; however, compared to the sweltering summers back home in northern Louisiana, today was still a mild day for MaryLou.

They sat at a shaded picnic table at the back of the house, each with a cold beer, a bowl of grapes and in the center of the table, and a small wheel of melted brie surrounded on a plate ringed with crackers.

"So, "Ethan started, "after all this time, it's good to see you. How you doing?"

"I'm ashamed I haven't come to see you sooner," she said. "Just been too busy."

"*What* are you doing? Tell me about your work."

"Well, you know, about my work. Typical nursing stuff. I switch between the OR and the ER every few months or so. The ER is actually more interesting, because of all the surprise afflictions that come in at all times of the night. I like the OR, though. The doctors actually tell jokes when they're working. Either that or how they're investing their money. And I work long hours. But what about you? How do you like Sonoma? I've never been up here, believe it or not."

"Pretty good. I haven't been as bored as I thought I would be, but still looking for a different job. You don't get wealthy selling cars up here and paying the rents."

"Yeah," she replied. "California is pretty ridiculous, I've found." She waved one arm at the surroundings. "But look at what we're paying for."

"Speaking of paying for, let me see this." Ethan grabbed her hand and began studying her engagement and wedding rings.

"Cassius told me you married a mechanic. I wouldn't imagine he had this kind of money."

"He doesn't. His family did though, at least they used to when they bought this a few decades ago. It's been in his family for a generation or two."

"I see, and how is married life treating you?"

"Fine," she said quickly, almost automatically.

He detected a note of finality to her tone. "Not really a glowing recommendation."

No, MaryLou thought to herself. But what was she going to do, tell her brother the truth? How sometimes she dreaded going home? Or that she could tell what type of mood he was in based on the number of beer cans or cigarette butts in the front seat of his car? Ethan had always been overly protective—he had to be, dealing with old Hiram's mercurial mentality—but also that wasn't going to help anything right now.

Ethan was staring at her. She realized she had been quiet for a while now. She opened up to speak but he cut her off.

"What is it, Mary? Do we have a problem at home?"

"No," she lied automatically again.

But by the look on his face, she knew she wasn't convincing him. He always knew when she was in trouble, the benefit of living so close and through so many difficult times as children.

Ethan leaned back in his chair.

"Maybe it's time I come visit you. You know, brother-in-law visits the happy couple?"

CHAPTER TWENTY-FIVE

I couldn't get out of the hospital fast enough. I raced to the street, almost injuring my other shoulder as I bumped into doors, people, and a countertop.

I pulled out my phone and dialed the last number I called.

"Ralston, Lombardi. I got something. Same place in thirty?"

"See you there."

What is it with some of these doctors today, I wondered as I drove out of the city center and thought about some of the cases I worked on in my past careers. Don't they make enough money?

I drove toward the less hectic Embarcadero and Bay and then straight to the Presidio and Liverpool Lil's to meet Bill.

I pulled into the same parking space I was in only a couple of days prior. Maybe Bill was at the same table—extra déjà vu.

He wasn't. He sat at the other side of the room this time, in front of a turkey club sandwich and sipping on a ginger ale.

"Still straight as ever, huh?"

"At least when I'm on duty," he replied as I sat down.

"No Keene?"

He shook his head. "Piled under with paperwork on another case. So, what do you have for me? To be perfectly honest, I need something."

I ordered the same sandwich as he had, but a glass of wine instead of the ginger ale.

"What's the one thing this case is missing?" I asked him.

"What do you mean?"

"We have murder. We have secret affairs. We have secret *secret* affairs. We have an abusive husband, father, the whole schmear, but what's the last piece to make this bingo card?"

"Beats me. I don't have time for this."

"Drugs," I said.

"Drugs?" he repeated it at first. Then looked at me. "DRUGS?"

"Yeah, turns out SF General had some doctor peddling opiates and pain killers under the table. Turns out a Dr. Ryan fellow was suspended for dealing opioids to patients—well after they should be off pain killers. And not just to patients, but out on the street as well."

I relayed what the doc had filled me in about the hospital keeping it hushed up, but that stories were swirling around that someone else on the staff was most likely involved. The doc went on to tell me that Dr. Ryan had been "on-leave" for a little over a week, but the staff all knew that meant fired.

I went on to tell Ralston, "So my source said he has been doing this for a while. Not super sophisticated, so not surprising it didn't take long to get found out."

"Yeah," he said. "How did the other shoe drop? Angry patient? Doctor?" I caught myself before saying my doc's name.

"Again, I haven't looked into this yet, but seems all this news about doctors across the country over-dealing these opiate drugs opened a large investigation in Sacramento, and they tracked him as one of the culprits here. So he wasn't even discovered locally, but once the staff here got word of his possible involvement, discovered his crime and that his medical license would be revoked, he was shown the door and he is lawyered up waiting for charges."

"Sounds like some great office gossip. I'll sic Keene on it."

"Think the kid can handle that?" I asked. I hadn't worked with Ralston's partner and was as yet unsure of his competence.

"He's an excellent guy for details. But what about MaryLou?" he said.

"Maybe," I said, "just maybe, our girl was thinking about blowing the whistle..."

Chapter Twenty-Six

I awoke later than usual. The sun was already over the ridge outside my living room window, signaling it was at least nine in the morning. In the upper canyons and ravines of Mill Valley on Mt. Tamalpais, the days can mimic towns above the arctic circle, where the steep gulleys can shield houses from sunlight for days at a time. That combined with heavy fog that searches for the lowest points to sit right above the ground creates a sense of isolation you can only break by walking out the door, starting the car, and descending back to civilization. Will the rest of the town be similarly foggy and cold, or sunny and balmy? You never knew until you got there, so a spare windbreaker, polo shirt, and shorts were requirements in the car's trunk as much as an ice scraper in a North Dakota winter.

Today was balmy. Lucky me. Once I got back in cell reception near the Buckeye restaurant by the 101 freeway, I called Bill to see if Harvey Keene could tie up some loose ends with the suspected drug dealing Dr. Ryan.

I pulled into the Buckeye's parking lot, a large white building hidden among some towering trees, though it's only about a five-iron away from the freeway exit. A quintessential Marin County dining mainstay with a cozy rustic bar and an Aspen lodge-style dining room adorned with vaulted ceilings and magnificent river-rock fireplace, the Buckeye Roadhouse was the type of place you go for a high school graduation or special date night. I had never been for breakfast, but I had to wait for Harvey to call me so I walked in and prayed they had some strong coffee and maybe a portable meal.

Harvey and I had agreed to meet in the Diamond Heights district in the city. Bill had filled him in on the details and he suggested we meet near the other side of Twin Peaks—apparently it was halfway and had a view. Houses there are the type where you have a postcard right outside your window.

Harvey was already pulled over a few blocks away from the address Bill gave. I wanted to strategize how to gather info on the suspect before I went to see him, as well as speak more to Harvey; I had never really worked with this guy, so I was going to size him up. My buddy Johnny was on the hook here, so yes, I needed to make sure the cops on the case were trustworthy and while I was fine with Ralston, Harvey Keene was a total unknown to me.

Harvey stepped out of the car; he was taller than I remembered from our first encounter. He got out, and got out, and kept getting out of his small Miata and approached holding a steaming cup of something. The typical aviators shielded his eyes from mine.

"Good morning, Lombardi," he welcomed me.

"Back at you. So tell me, what are we looking at with this Ryan guy?" I shot back. Straight to business. I had been on this case long enough I felt I had to get some resolution for my pal Johnny.

"Well, pretty much what I told Bill on the phone. I need to look into this more, but briefly, Dr. Ryan came from a middle-class family in Youngstown, Ohio, where his father worked at U.S. Steel. Private high school, degree from Ohio State, first in Chemical Engineering, then to University of Michigan Medical School. Internships locally in California and a specialty in thoracic surgery followed by a brief stint at a hospital in Sacramento. He married a fellow student in medical school, but divorced her. Had been at San Francisco General for seven years, recently re-married to an aspiring opera singer, and now lived in a palatial house in the oh-so-exclusive Pacific Heights neighborhood. He's been 'on-leave' for two and a half weeks, but we all know that means fired."

"Right."

"Seems there was an investigation and they tracked him as one of the dealers. But once the hospital here discovered his crime and that his medical license would be revoked, he was shown the door and he is lawyered up fighting it."

"Well, he probably won't have much to say, but maybe a murder charge can get him talking."

Harvey took off his sunglasses now. "I think you can be convincing." Harvey was definitely the type of cop you do not want against you. I was starting to see why Bill chose him as a partner.

I was about to go when Harvey asked if I had a minute to follow him to his place. There was something he wanted to show me. We decided instead to take his car. Harvey lived in a house on a hill in Brisbane that appeared to have been built in the seventies, the type of place you don't buy for the house, but for the view. It was just over the San Francisco county line, but overlooked the bay rather than the ocean.

We walked up several flights of stairs to his front door and Harvey wrapped loudly in a way all cops somehow know how to do. Maybe they teach intimidating door knocking nowadays at the academy?

"Why are you knocking at your own door?" I asked.

"Not my house anymore. Actually, getting divorced but some of my boxes are still here. The ex knows we're swinging by."

The door opened to an almost middle-aged, average-looking woman in the entrance. She looked at us, waiting for our reason for disturbing her. Maybe Harvey hadn't alerted her after all, but either way, it was his turn to take the lead.

"May we come in?" Harvey asked, but it was more of a statement.

"Yeah," the ex-wife replied, just as gruffly.

"This is my associate," he gestured to me. "Steve Lombardi." This would normally be the part when he introduced himself and flashed his badge way too fast for anyone to register. Why do they always do that? But his introduction was not needed.

I nodded to her, flashed a smile, but she didn't smile back. I felt invisible.

Harvey continued, "I want to show him a picture I have in one of my boxes real quick. We'll be out of here in a few minutes."

She didn't say anything but stepped aside, letting us into the dimly lit house. Seems their time for small talk was well past.

I was obviously flustered, but Harvey smiled at me as we stepped down into his sunken living room. It had to be the original carpeting, I thought. The view even was obstructed by some overgrown eucalyptus trees. Quite the disappointment.

Harvey walked me to a seating area and told me to wait. He returned a second later, with a photograph, framed, with young rookie Bill Ralston and Johnny Lynch smiling. He said he saw this in Lynch's office at headquarters after he was placed on leave and wanted to give it back to him.

"Maybe you want to give it to him? Tell him with my compliments? Maybe make him feel better about working with me."

I looked down at a younger friend of mine, embracing his still younger colleague.

What the hell happened? I thought.

"Thank you," I told Harvey. "I'm sure he'll be glad he has you on our side."

"There are no sides, Lombardi, only one. Justice. I think we all need to understand that."

I nodded. I felt better myself.

CHAPTER TWENTY-SEVEN

After retrieving my car, I met Ralston for lunch and filled him in on what Keene had told me. I asked if he wanted to visit this Dr. Ryan with me, but he declined, reminding me that this was a criminal investigation, after all, and showing up together might complicate things if it ever came to a court trial.

"You and I are not working with each other on this case," is the way he put it. "And because we're not, and don't even know each other, we certainly aren't sharing any information with each other."

"Certainly not," I said, knowing full well what he was saying and realizing I should have known better than to even ask him.

"Besides," he said after sipping his ginger ale, "I have a dentist's appointment that's going to put me out of commission for the rest of the day and probably tomorrow."

"Sounds terrible," I said.

"I don't even want to think about it," he said. "They want to pull out two wisdom teeth at one sitting."

"Ouch."

"Call me as soon as you interview the doc," he said.

I looked at my watch and changed my mind. "First thing tomorrow," I said. "I think I'll take the rest of today to run up and talk to MaryLou's brother."

"Good luck," he said. "We didn't get anything remarkable out of him and I doubt if he's involved."

We clinked glasses and I left him with the remaining half of my sandwich.

And the bill.

The water of a raging river always looks fastest from the banks. Ethan Fitzgerald was familiar with that expression—it was what prompted him to enlist in the Navy the day he finally turned seventeen. That, and "Join the Navy and See the World," the same slogan that romanced the young Steve Lombardi to do the same thing. Ethan was also convinced it was the quickest way to get out of the shack he grew up in and get out from under his father's thumb. Up to that day life seemed slow and eventless, his decisions made as quickly as a turtle stampeding through peanut butter.

The Thanksgiving of his junior year in high school was the final straw. He and Hiram had had yet another shouting match that was almost turning violent when he gathered up what clothing he could and raced out the door, hoping never to walk back through it again. He felt bad leaving his younger sister, but he couldn't help her until he first helped himself.

He had contemplated his options, even discussed them with MaryLou, who, even as a sophomore Ethan knew was way sharper than himself. Straight A's in school, and all that, knowing already that she would go to college and become a nurse. He was always interested in mechanics, fixing the family tractor being his favorite chore. But there wasn't much future in that career. He also had an empathetic heart, which led to investigate becoming an EMT in the fire department. But after discovering how much training was required, he crossed that off the list as well. Also crossed off was law enforcement, after hearing disparaging stories told by his football teammates about police brutality against Black people.

Then he discovered the military. The Army was a popular choice among the youth of Caddo Parish, but trudging through muck and mire in the rain didn't seem quite as exhilarating as the fresh air of the open seas. In the Navy he trained as an aircraft mechanic on aircraft carriers, with tours that took him to Subic Bay in the Philippines, around the Cape Horn at Tierra del Fuego, the South China Sea, and the expansive Indian Ocean, where the

U.S.S. John F. Kennedy patrolled mostly between Sri Lanka and the horn of Africa. He didn't see any combat action, although he repaired a chopper that had received a lot of ground fire off the Somali coast in a rescue mission. After five tours and ten years of service, he finally decided to forget about a Navy pension and he mustered out at northern California's Treasure Island, prepared for a landlocked life.

Northern California, while worlds apart from his home in the deep south, had the same anonymous back roads he grew up driving on, small towns out in the farm lands between coastal hills and ocean, undiscovered by highways or tourists. Ethan enjoyed renting a motorcycle and exploring Sonoma Valley, stopping at small wine tasting rooms or ramshackle country markets along the way.

Sonoma is just north of what is called the "Bay Area," technically part of the seven-county region, but one could be forgiven for feeling totally disconnected from the rest of the metropolitan area or the Los Angeles-like population of the East Bay across from San Francisco. Sonoma Valley runs parallel to her more famous sister to the east, Napa Valley of "Most Happy Fella" fame. However, Sonoma's vineyards and wines are just as celebrated, even as its more rural and affordable neighborhoods attracted younger families looking for starter homes and space, people willing to pay for land rather than a zip code. Even on his meager Navy pay savings, Ethan felt comfortably middle class in Sonoma and became attracted to the town of Santa Rosa.

He began checking out job opportunities on his motorcycle rides, stopping at auto body shops, the few regional airports, the larger agricultural and ranching operations, hoping they had a need for a trained mechanic on their payroll. But he was a victim of bad timing. The recent fires that had rampaged throughout the area had devastated the housing and employment picture, and money and jobs had begun to migrate south to Marin County and the East Bay. Locals parsed through their charred belongings, desperate figures roaming amid the surviving brick chimneys standing like a forest of stalagmites amid the ruins.

On a whim, Ethan stopped at a Ford dealership that, while not in need of mechanics, was building a new staff of younger salesmen. It just happened that the owner's son had just mustered out of the Coast Guard and, as part of his inherited supervisory training, was now the sales manager. He was sympathetic to Ethan's Navy experience and search for employment, and hired him on the spot.

Ethan was settled into a routine before he heard about his sister's marital issues. They weren't rumors and she didn't confide in him, but they were brought to his attention in his infrequent chats with Cassius. Ethan was always protective of his sister, but never one to get in her way, to make decisions for her. She had lived just as long as he had, if not a year longer, with their father. She could handle herself. But after their chat when she visited him in Santa Rosa, his feelings toward her reverted back to their school days, and he saw something needed to be done.

When I called, Ethan Fitzgerald didn't want to talk with me at the Santa Rosa Ford dealership, claiming he'd already been interviewed by police investigators and had nothing more to contribute. I convinced him I had been hired by a friend falsely accused and that I would not ask him to do anything illegal or compose any lies. He finally consented and suggested we meet for a drink after his shift at 5 p.m. at a smallish Thai restaurant in Old Town Santa Rosa, which was about an hour's drive from Mill Valley.

As usual, I arrived a little early to get my bearings and check the place out. I don't know why, but it's my usual habit when I enter a place I've never been before to check out the men's room, note the location of all exits and, if possible, sit at the last place at the bar with my back to the wall. Call it paranoia. Or maybe I've seen too many western movies.

He was a good-looking kid—no surprise there—with hair not quite as red as his sister's, but red enough to make his ancestry obvious. I guessed late twenties, maybe just turned thirty. Tall, good build, clean shaven, obviously took care of himself, and a neat dresser: grey slacks, blue blazer and a yellow knit tie over a light blue button-down collar shirt. Probably the suggested attire for selling cars.

He slid onto his seat and we shook hands. He ordered a beer.

"Thanks for meeting me," I said. "I'm sorry about your loss."

"Damn tragic," he said. "I can't believe they're calling it murder." He squinted his eyes at me. "What happened to your face?"

I had to smile. "I know," I said. "I look like Jake LaMotta."

"Who's Jake LaMotta?"

Now I had to laugh out loud. "Forget it. Let's just say I had an argument with a friend."

Now he laughed. "Jeez. Don't ever get into an argument with an enemy!"

Where do these comedians get their writers?

"Were you and MaryLou close?" I asked.

A shrug. "Not really," he said. "I was only a year older than her, but we ran in different circles. She was extremely bright in school. I worked like hell to get Cs."

"How did you both end up here?" I asked. "Did she follow you?"

He shook his head and took a pull on his bottle. "Nah. I joined the Navy the day I turned seventeen and was stationed first in San Diego and then did several tours overseas. I loved working on carriers and re-upped a few times, then I mustered out over in the East Bay at Treasure Island. I loved the North Bay so I stayed. It was a total coincidence she ended up in San Francisco. She'd always wanted to get the hell out of Louisiana."

"She didn't know you were here?"

"She did. I'd send her an email now and then, but I had nothing to do with her moving here." He looked up at the ceiling, as if thinking. "In fact, at first I'd only spoken to her once on the phone. She called to tell me she was getting married and not to be pissed that I wasn't invited to the wedding. She said it was a small thing up in Tahoe."

"Didn't you think that strange?"

"Not really. I was on deployment and hadn't been able to see her at all after I enlisted. I just said congrats, you know, good luck, and no sweat. It didn't bother me at all."

"Why did you join the Navy?" I smiled. "Sounds like you didn't like Louisiana either."

"Remember that old slogan about 'seeing the world'?"

I lifted my glass in a toast as I grinned. "Worked on me too, "I said. "Better-looking uniforms, too."

He laughed. "Uh-oh," he said. "You must have been an officer."

I toasted again. "Better food, too."

I continued, "NorCal is quite different than your upbringing."

His expression suddenly changed. He took another pull and his eyes grew dark, serious. "Mooringsport? Couldn't stand it. Hated school, hated the weather, hated the place we lived in."

"So what brought you to Santa Rosa?"

"As I said, I was stationed at Treasure Island when I mustered out, got to exploring Marin County, especially over on the coast, and fell in love with it. I couldn't afford the rents in Corte Madera or San Rafael, which I *really* liked, but I soon found that here in Sonoma county everything was cheap enough."

I nodded in agreement. We both felt the same about Marin, but I had been fortunate enough to get in cheap. "How did you get into selling cars?"

"It was the first job I could find. I didn't learn much in the Navy besides how to fix things, worked in different details, not just aircraft engines, but I liked communications and got interested in computers. I'm going to night school now. Learning computer science."

I smiled. "Still getting Cs?"

He laughed. "You got it, man. Just enough to pass."

"I've heard your father was tough on you kids."

"He was a sonofabitch. A wild-ass, drunken, bigoted sono-foabitch." His eyes grew dark again.

It was my turn to shake my head. "Jeez," I said.

"Sorry," he said. "I try not to think about him."

"The cops are trying to find him, but he's disappeared. I presume you haven't heard from him"

"Not since I got out. They think he had something to do with MaryLou?"

"A 'person of interest,' as they say. Was he a violent sort?"

Now a cynical nod. "Oh, yeah. When he got drunk, there wasn't a person, place or thing that was spared his rage. He'd curse at the TV screen. Throw things. Lots of times we'd hide in the closet until he passed out. MaryLou told me he even crashed her high school prom and tried to strangle her date, Cassius. He's a good guy, also now lives in the area. I'd never heard a thing about it until she told me about it much later."

"Do you think Hiram is capable of murder?"

He threw up his hands. "I don't know. He's explosive enough. But why? Why would he come all the way out here to kill his daughter? She told me she hadn't even spoken to him since she graduated high school. He couldn't even know where she lived. Nah, it couldn't be him. Why would he even give a damn? Besides, I can't think of a single person we ever knew who didn't think the world of her. I can't imagine *anyone* doing that."

"Was that Cassius the same kid she's still friends with? An engineer down the Peninsula?"

"Yeah, Cassius. He and I stayed in occasional touch over the years. Mostly email." He chuckled. "He kept me more informed about MaryLou than she did. I didn't know anything about her work, or her social life. You know, that personal stuff."

"But you knew she got married," I said.

Now he grew serious again, nodded. "Yeah, as I told you, she called to tell me why I wasn't invited to the wedding. No big deal. Cassius told me she married a guy she hardly knew. Stunned everyone. He said all her friends wondered about it. I forget his name."

"Walter."

"Yeah, that's it. She came up to visit me a while ago. I'm not quite sure why, probably just out of sibling obligation. But when I asked her how everything was going with the husband she really clammed up."

"She wouldn't talk about it?" I asked.

"Nope. 'Fine,' was all she'd say and change the subject."

"Some psychologists would suggest that's what they call a 'cry for help'," I said.

He shrugged. "Maybe. I hinted I could go down there and visit. At least meet the guy, but she never extended the invite."

"Did it sound like she was afraid of him?"

"Maybe a hint," he said. "As I said, we dropped the subject."

"Any chance she was fooling around?"

His eyes lit up. "How the hell would *I* know?" he said. "But I guess it's always a possibility. She was pretty strait-laced. I always thought she didn't date around much from some of her emails from college. But, yeah, it's always a possibility, I guess."

"So, you wouldn't know anything about her sex life?"

He chuckled again. "Are you kidding?"

"Would it surprise you that she was bisexual?"

Now a real laugh. "No! Really?" He seemed more startled than surprised. "Hah! Yes, I'm damn surprised." Then he shrugged again. "But I don't know why I should be. She's ... was ... a gorgeous girl. It's her choice, after all."

"She was having an affair with the friend who hired me, a guy, but she was also seeing a woman named Cindy."

"Was she still married to that brute? The asshole? I haven't seen anything in the papers. Are they keeping it quiet?"

I nodded. "The guy she was seeing is a cop." I paused. "Her marriage wasn't working. But how did you know that?"

He blinked at me. "What? Know what?"

"That he was an asshole? You called him a brute. How did you know that, if you didn't know anything about him and hardly ever spoke with her?"

"Oh." He shrugged again and looked at his empty bottle and turned it around a few times. "I guess she must've mentioned it in an email, or something."

I nodded. "Or something," I said.

"Sounds like he's your suspect, though, if you ask me."

"What if your father found out about the female lover? Or Cassius being out here with her."

He shook his head. "He'd go berserk. But I can't imagine how he'd ever know about either one."

"Unless someone tipped him off," I said.

He just nodded again a few times. "I suppose," he said softly.

He suddenly finished his beer and got up to go. I offered to buy him another beer, but he begged off, saying he had to get back to work and didn't want beer on his breath. I wanted to mention that I thought his shift was over, but I thought better of it. I thanked him again, gave him my card, and asked him to call me if he thought of anything that might be important to the case. I watched him go out the door and, suddenly feeling like a snack, ordered another glass of wine and reached for a menu. I went through the strange and yet very appetizing-sounding Thai names, like *Kra Prow* and *Yum Pla Muk* and *Pad Prik Khing*. I wasn't especially hungry after my half-club lunch, but on the dinner menu I saw a tempting "small plate" that translated into "Coconut Macadamia Nut Shrimp with tempura and mango mojo." The interesting mix of spices and ingredients made it well worth a try.

While it was coming, I stared down into my wine, reflecting on my meeting with Ethan. Something just didn't sit right with the conversation we'd just had. The kid seemed honest enough, forthcoming, but the thing about him knowing the husband might be roughing her up didn't sound right. Sure, maybe MaryLou did mention it to him sometime during one of their rare communications. Or maybe someone else told him. But who else knew about it? For that matter, it made me wonder: What if someone *did* tip off the much-disliked father, and he got so riled he came to San Francisco in his Irish rage and wasted MaryLou himself. But how?

He certainly wasn't sleeping with her. Did he sneak up from behind, as Ralston suggested to Dr. Feinberg? And, yes, he would certainly be dumb enough to think she was dead and throw her off the bridge. And who was the subject of the tip-off? The jilted childhood friend? Johnny Lynch himself? The Cindy thing?

Any one of them could have lit the old guy's short fuse.

CHAPTER TWENTY-EIGHT

The next morning was wet. Not because it had rained but from the dew and mist that hung over the mountain, feeding the redwoods and sequoias enough water to allow them to reach the heavens. Moving through the mist left you with beads of water all over your clothes and could fog your glasses. That is, if you wore them.

I wanted to call John just to check-in and to tell him what I was up to. We hadn't spoken since the "altercation" but he might pick up. I hadn't told him about the revelation about Dr. Ryan and thought it was a good idea to do so before my interview. I wondered whether MaryLou had ever mentioned anything about the opioid rumor to him.

I decided to use one of the last payphones in the county to hide my identity and see if John would finally answer a call. Sure enough, he did.

I decided to get right to the point to avoid giving him a chance to hang up on me in case there was any lingering animosity. At the end of the day, friends or not, he was a client involved in a murder investigation. And he understood the gravity of that situation more than most.

I could tell he didn't want to speak to me yet, but we got down to business.

He was surprised when I mentioned Dr. Ryan. "Nah," he said, "never said a word. If there was anything illegal going on, I'd bet my pension she had nothing to do with it."

"I figured since you were a cop, she'd confide in you. You know, ask your advice on whether to blow the whistle."

"We never talked about work much," John said. "I guess it was kind of an unspoken taboo not to talk about work or her marriage."

"Did she ever mention a Dr. Ryan? He was allegedly dealing it and got suspended for it. All hush-hush, though."

"No, and I never heard a word about that. They must have done a helluva job keeping it secret."

"I'm going over to see him this morning," I said. "Ralston didn't know anything about it, either."

"You know he's not going to talk to you."

"He might if he's innocent. He'll be pretty pissed off at the hospital."

"No way," John said. "My money says yeah, he's pissed off, but he's probably planning a lawsuit, so he's not talking to anyone but his mouthpiece."

I took a deep breath. "Did MaryLou ever mention that she dated him a few times?"

He said nothing for a brief moment. "No, but that must have been before we met. She wasn't seeing anyone after that."

I exhaled and decided to leave it alone. Even though he couldn't sock me over the radio waves, there was no sense mentioning Cindy.

"OK, pal. I'll let you know what he says. Hang in there."

"You too," he said, and hung up before I did.

I checked my watch and decided to stop by the Buckeye one more time for more coffee and a bear claw since I had the time.

I decided to just show up at Dr. Ryan's door and check if my luck was getting any better. Ralston's partner Keene didn't find any police record on him, not even a parking ticket, so I figured SF General was doing a good job of keeping his dismissal quiet. When I called Lucy Reynolds, she couldn't remember MaryLou ever mentioning

SCOTT ADDEO YOUNG AND EDMOND G. ADDEO

Ryan's name, nor did she apparently even suggest anything was going on with illegal opioid drugs.

Pacific Heights has often been called the most expensive neighborhood in the United States and, yes, that includes Beverly Hills and Martha's Vineyard. The locals call it "Billionaires' Row," with homes selling for more than $4,000 a square foot and featuring a Chamber of Commerce mural right outside every available window, including the bathrooms. Dr. Ryan's "house" was a corner Victorian mansion with a spectacular view of the Golden Gate Bridge and San Francisco Bay.

It made me wonder if he could actually afford this just by sewing people up. He certainly couldn't be paying the first wife any alimony. Maybe the second wife, the opera singer, was one of the Rockefeller granddaughters.

My first surprise was that the large spiked iron gate in the front wasn't locked, but opened freely when I turned the ancient handle. I walked up a smooth brick path through a superbly manicured lawn and garden, and up three marble steps into a *porte-cochere* kind of structure meant to keep visitors out of the wind and rain. To my right was a bronze-rimmed intercom set with a mother-of-pearl buzzer, and a TV camera on a swivel-mounted above it. I pushed the buzzer as I checked my watch: 10:30 on the nose.

A faint female voice replied with a simple, "Yes?"

"Is Dr. Ryan available, please?"

"Who is calling?"

I took out my wallet and held my ID and driver's license up to the TV camera. "My name is Steve Lombardi. I'm a private investigator."

Silence for a long moment. "And what is your business, please?"

"I have important business I'd like to discuss with Dr. Ryan, if I may." I folded my wallet back up and gave the camera my most endearing smile.

Now a longer silence and a different, younger, female voice came on.

"This is Mrs. Ryan. Who are you and what do you want? Dr. Ryan is very busy."

I doubted that, but kept the smile pasted to my face. "I know I don't have an appointment but this could be urgent. It's about his work at San Francisco General. Would you tell him it concerns a nurse he worked with? A MaryLou Kowalski?"

Yet another silence. Then a gruff, "Just a second."

After another wait, some muffled voices, rustling as a phone or whatever it was got passed around. Then, a strong baritone voice, with an urgency of its own.

"This is Dr. Ryan. Are you a reporter?"

"No, sir. I'm a private investigator as I explained to your secretary. I'm working on the MaryLou Kowalski case."

"What about her? What do you mean, 'case'?" he said.

He hadn't heard yet. He must have been really laying low.

"I guess you haven't heard yet, doctor. She's been murdered."

In a mini-second the lock release buzzed on the heavy door in front of me. I opened it and stepped directly into a large mahogany-paneled living room, with Persian rugs, antique Tiffany lamps, beveled glass mirrors, and tables and, immediately to my right, a curved, carpeted stairway down which bounded a tall, tanned, athletic-looking man taking the stairs two at a time. I thought briefly about how much more difficult that was going down than up, and I pegged him as a tennis player.

He approached me quickly and offered his hand. "You certainly know how to get a man's attention," he said. "I'm Dr. Ryan."

I shook his hand. "Steve Lombardi. I'm sorry to barge in like this."

We stepped down into his bright living room. It had to be recently remodeled I thought. His view was also rudely interrupted by several large eucalyptus trees. Another disappointment.

I had virtually the same opinion of Harvey Keene's obstructed view at his ... well, *former* home.

He showed me to a love seat and took a straight-backed chair directly opposite. "I hope I didn't hear you right. You said MaryLou was *murdered?*"

I nodded. "It happened last week. It's been meticulously hushed up because the main suspect is a San Francisco cop she'd been seeing. He's an old friend of mine who swears he's innocent and I'm helping him out."

He sat back and ran both hands through a full head of curly black hair. "Hold on, hold on," he said. "You're throwing a lot of information at me all at once. How was she murdered and who is this cop friend of yours?"

I shook my head and smiled. "Sorry, doc. She was found in McCovey Cove apparently drowned but there wasn't any water in her lungs. I'm sure you understand the implication."

"Of course, of course," he nodded. "So you said she was having an affair with this cop? She was married, right?"

"Yes, she was. And naturally her husband is also a suspect. But with all respect, Dr. Ryan, I can't really go into a lot of details. I have to respect that it's a criminal investigation and my client's— the cop's—privileged information."

He nodded again. "Yes, I get it. We have confidentiality in our business as well. But what's all that have to do with me?"

"Is it true that you once dated MaryLou?"

He leaned back now, relaxing. "Yes, but only twice. And we were both single then."

"I see. And I understand you've been laid off recently. Something about illegal opioid dealing?"

I fully expected an angry reaction, or at least something resembling resentment. But he smiled, interlocking his fingers across his stomach. "And when did you hear about that, Mr. Lombardi?"

"Just recently," I said. "The police don't know about it yet."

Now he leaned forward. "And why should they? I'm afraid you may have jumped the gun, sir. If you'd spoken to the hospital administration before coming here, you'd know that I've been fully exonerated. There is no truth to the allegations whatsoever, and I resume my duties at General when I come back from a brief vacation in Cabo San Lucas next week."

"Well, congratulations then," I said with genuine relief. "So there was no such 'illegal drugs' going on?"

"None at all," he said. "I was simply passing a few opioid-based drugs to former patients in great pain but who couldn't afford them. Free samples, if you wish. No prescriptions needed. Happens all the time. This wasn't even that recent or local; it was from years ago when I was at UC Davis." He sat back and shook his head in mock disgust. "I don't know how these stupid rumors get started. Or why they pick back up."

"The question came up whether MaryLou was involved," I said. "And naturally when she turned up murdered…"

"Another stupid conjecture!" he almost shouted. "Just because we dated a few times a few years ago?"

He had a flash of anger wipe across his face, but it dissipated instantly. Seemed like a man who has had to explain himself a lot recently. I understood the frustration.

"Why do you think these rumors re-circulate?"

He leaned forward. "You know, I'm not sure. With all the over-prescription of Oxy and other opioids and various barbiturates in the news right now I am sure it is just one of those things that sticks. Topical. But that is just my guess, maybe I need to hire you as a P.I. once this case is over to get to the bottom of it."

He was charismatic too. Some guys just have all the luck—house in Pac Heights, Opera singer wife. Not even bald, damn him.

I stood up and extended my hand. "Well, I'm glad it's all resolved," I said. "I'm happy for both your *and* MaryLou's reputation."

He patted me on the back as he walked me to the doorway. "If I can be of any help, please call me," he said. "She was a nice girl and an excellent nurse."

"Thank you, doctor," I said. "By the way, I understand your wife's an opera singer."

"Yes," he grinned. "She is, and pretty good too. My unbiased opinion, of course."

I laughed. "Of course. Can I see her perform anywhere in town?"

He shook his head in the doorway. "Not at present. She's auditioning for a few parts, though. 'Mimi' in "La Boheme" next month. And a smaller part in "Turandot" in San Jose."

"I'll watch for her," I said. "Thanks again."

And he closed the door.

CHAPTER TWENTY-NINE

John Lynch was first-generation Irish—and always made a point to bring it up—the only son of Sean Lynch from Cork and Eileen Brennan from Cobh, an island in the middle of Cork Harbor. (Cobh is the Celtic spelling, pronounced "Cove".) Sean was an avid sailor, plying the waters off the harbor and entering every regatta the Cork Yacht Club staged. It was his preference not to hang out at the club, however, preferring instead the cozy bar in the Continental Hotel on the waterfront in Cobh. And since Eileen's father was the harbormaster, it wasn't long before the two of them met and spent practically every weekend wining and dining and sailing far out into the ocean past the breakers. Most folks don't realize that Cork Harbor is the second-largest natural harbor in the world, after Sydney Harbor in Australia. In fact, was also the place where courageous Cork fisherman rescued both the living and the dead after the *RMS Lusitania*, a British ocean liner, was torpedoed on 7 May 1915 by a German U-boat eleven miles off the harbor, partially instigating the United States declaration of war on Germany two years later. And also again, it was the last berth from which the *Titanic* sailed.

When they were married and rented a small place on Cobh, Sean began working for Eileen's father, and after two years, when Sean secured a job working for the Harbor Authority in San Francisco, he and Eileen crossed the Atlantic for America, taking the time to go via the Panama Canal and up the Honduran, Guatemalan, El Salvadoran, Costa Rican, Mexican and California coasts to San

Francisco. John Lynch never missed an opportunity to brag that he was conceived on that crossing.

He was born in the old French Hospital on Geary Street, raised in the Marina neighborhood and, in a typical Irish Catholic upbringing went to St. Ignatius High School and the University of San Francisco. His four years in the U.S. Army's Military Police convinced him to join the SF police department upon his discharge.

I pulled into oncoming traffic past one of the many blind turns in the Pacific Heights neighborhood of the City. After interviewing Dr. Ryan, I was in a rush to see Johnny. On the way I had called him once again, got no answer, and headed straight for his apartment on Nob Hill.

Strangely, I had never been to any of John's apartments. Now that I thought about it, I couldn't even tell you why. When he was just a rookie cop he lived in a small apartment in the Sunset District, which was affordable then, and throughout his uniform years he rented a small bachelor pad off Bay Street near the Columbus Avenue intersection. And I had visited that only once, and even then, I had hardly got through the door when he snatched his hat and sped us on our way to wherever we were headed. All I remember was a big LeRoy Neiman print of Willie Mays on his living room wall.

After he made Inspector, John moved to a nice smallish bachelor pad on Russian Hill with a sweeping view of the whole City, very upper class that absolutely no cops with families could afford. He often mentioned a spectacular view of the bay and the Golden Gate Bridge. Or so he said—for some inexplicable reason I had never seen this place, either. Even when we were partners, we'd always arrange to meet in some bar or restaurant or, especially when working, in a coffee shop or a small Greek place hard by our headquarters on Bryant Street. Now, I even wondered why I knew his address.

My luck was holding as I found a parking spot on upper Jones, and hiked up to his building on Sacramento. The vestibule, of course, was enclosed with a series of mailboxes, under each of which was a phony pearl button to summon the occupants.

Dead end. If he wouldn't answer his phone, why the hell would he answer a buzz from an unknown visitor? It only took me a moment to remember to repeat the buzz with the old "shave-and-a-haircut" rhythm, hopefully to show him it was someone friendly.

No response. I buzzed again, the same rhythm, and waited some more.

Still nothing. I tried it a third time. I figured by now he had to think it was someone he knew. Suddenly the intercom buzzed.

"Yes?" it said.

"You want to go for round two?" I said.

Silence. Then, "Shit."

"I've hired a new ref?" I said, with a questioning inflection.

"Shit," again, which I took as an apologetic repetition.

"Hit the fucking buzzer, John!"

And it buzzed. I flipped open the door and went to the elevator that took me to the oh-so-exclusive top floor. I fleetingly wondered—as I had several times—whether John had inherited some money from the enterprising late parents from Cork Harbor, money that he hadn't mentioned before, as close as we were. The Marina District, where they'd lived, had been soaring in real estate value. Then again, as close as we were, there was a lot I didn't really know about my best friend John Lynch.

The doors opened, and I walked out onto a plush corridor carpet that led me hesitantly to apartment 9B.

The door wasn't open. One would think an expected guest, in the time it took from downstairs buzzer to top-floor elevator, would be greeted by a welcoming visitee at an open door down the hallway.

I stopped at the door, waiting for an open greeting.

Nothing. I knocked.

The door slowly opened and John, unshaven, in rumpled trousers and a shirt that looked like he barely survived a wrestling match with the head of a silverback gorilla family, looked at me.

I said nothing, but knew he was taking in my once-salmon-but-now-eggplant-colored cheek.

"Stevie," he said, with eyes suddenly bursting wet. He took a long step forward, arms outstretched, and I stepped forward to join him. We hugged silently, swaying back and forth, for a long time. We said nothing.

Still hugging, still silent, he backed us into the room, kicked the door shut, and clung on for long minutes.

"Hey, man," I said. "Don't worry about it. Shit happens."

He sniffed, slowly, and reluctantly I thought, stepped out of the embrace. "Jesus, what can I say?"

I said, "You can say, 'what are you drinking?'"

He managed a smile, turned and walked to a small bar in a corner of his living room.

The room was small, as I expected, but totally adequate for a single guy with a good income. On one wall above a tan leather recliner was the LeRoy Neiman "Willie Mays" print I remembered. In another corner was a desk with a short return, apparently where he spends most of his working time. The desk held a 24-inch screen iMac computer, an all-in-one color Brother printer to the left, a landline phone, assorted electrical wires, and a library-style brass lamp, with five outlet connects. To the right hung a corkboard with various notes, pictures of who-knows-who, an upright holder with several folders inserted, a utility rack with pens, highlighters, scissors, magnifying glass, Sharpies, a small Giants pennant, and miscellaneous ballpoints and red markers strewn about the desktop. Above the computer was a 180-degree photo of the ballpark now called Oracle Park but featuring a big PacBell sign in the picture. Some photos of kids and a few women I didn't recognize, an SFPD Silver Medal of Valor plaque, and a few kinds of military ribbons I couldn't identify dangling from a large green "Kiss Me, I'm Irish" button. To the right was a galley kitchen, on the left a door that I presumed led to a bedroom.

In the first corner was a small table that I figured served as a dinette of some sort, with two captain's chairs on each side. He obviously never hosted a dinner party.

That seemed to be it.

Something made me turn and look back at the desk corner. A hunch suddenly struck me—a longshot, true, but nevertheless a strong one.

John came back from the bar corner with a tumbler of scotch over ice, handed it to me, and indicated the two captain's chairs. We sat, still not having said another word, and he raised his glass offering a toast. I raised mine.

We just clinked. He was at a loss for words, so I said, "To friendship."

"Jesus," he said again.

"Hey, man. Taking the Lord's name in vain isn't getting us anywhere."

"I'm just so fucking sorry, Stevie," he said. "I don't know what I was thinking."

"You *weren't* thinking, that's all. You went into some kind of frenzy. The news was a big shock, I know. But let's go on from there, OK?"

He nodded, raised his glass again. "How did the chat with the doctor go?"

"Dead end, nothing new we need to look into. Still need to find this mysterious Cindy though."

"How did you find out about her?"

"As I tried to tell you then," I said, "the hideout roommate told me. Lucy. They worked together at the hospital and I gather they exchanged a lot of personal information. Don't you remember I told you the other woman's name was Cindy?"

He shook his head. "No, not really," he said. Then, hesitantly, "The tattoo?"

"Right."

149

"How can you be sure it's true?"

"It's pretty vague. I know," I said. "But she had no reason to make it up, to lie about it. She's got no skin in the game." I paused. "So to speak."

He didn't crack a smile.

"And she couldn't have known about the tattoo," I went on. "So she couldn't have pulled the name out of thin air."

"That's still no proof," he said.

I shrugged. "All I can think of now is to track her down and confront her with it."

"Slim chance," he said. "No last name, no real proof it was even her real name." He took a slug of scotch and looked out the window. "And I'll bet there are half a dozen gay Cindys out here in the city."

"I'm debating whether to tell Bill Ralston." I said. "He's probably combing the city bars already."

"Fat chance," he said. "Experienced bartenders can smell a cop half a block away."

Another swig.

"But no, I wouldn't tell him. Find her yourself."

I nodded. "Will do," I said. "And by the way, you still owe me a dinner."

This time I got an ever-so-slight smile. He looked at his watch. "How about now?" he said.

I got up. "You got a deal."

"Lemme go change," he said, as he jerked a jacket from his closet and disappeared down the hall.

As he did so I quickly stepped to the desk and looked it over once more. Something about it bothered me.

"Where to?" he said as he reappeared, much better dressed. "Since it's my treat you get to pick."

"Tadich Grill," I said. "I feel like being abused by an impudent waiter."

⚜ ⚜ ⚜

CHAPTER THIRTY

Trying not to look like an undercover cop wasn't easy. I don't have a beard or a mustache, so I can't look too scraggly. I don't own dirty, worn out shoes and the only jeans I wear are nearly new. And all—or most—of the undercover guys I've met are tasked with associating among the lowest scumbags that walk the earth, so they almost *have* to look scraggly and dirty.

On the other hand, trying not to look like a cop in plain clothes is also impossible. A plain clothes cop wears—you got it: *plain clothes!* Jeans and sweat shirt? Check. Slacks and open collar shirt? Check. Sweat suit? Tennis outfit? Blue blazer and white turtle neck? How about cowboy shirt and boots? Check, check, check, check and *yee-haw.*

You get the point. I opted for my clean jeans, loafers, a Giants t-shirt and my Notre Dame windbreaker—go Irish!

Neither Johnny nor I could figure out how to find the mysterious (and, yes, alleged) person named "Cindy," but we both agreed the best place to start looking was at a few saloons noted to be queer hangouts. But with a more accepting climate for our fellow LGBTQ+ citizens, there no longer seemed to be specific bars that were exclusively frequented by homosexual and trans patrons. But John mentioned as a starting point a small joint in the outer Mission District called Alice B's. It didn't take a lot of pondering to figure it was named after Gertrude Stein's famous lesbian partner Alice B. Toklas, but most people probably don't know that Toklas was born on O'Farrell Street in San Francisco, or that in 1989 the city's notoriously whacky Board of Supervisors dedicated a block of Myrtle Street between Polk and Van Ness as Alice B. Toklas Place.

So I thought I'd start with Alice B's and headed back over the bridge. But this time I parked on Bay and took an Uber ride to the Outer Mission district. I know I'm always whining about it, but traffic in town these days is to be avoided at all costs and I didn't feel like spending an hour to cross town, incessantly waiting behind delivery trucks, construction detours, red lights and PG&E jackhammer jockeys. So I had my poor driver do that part.

I gave the Uber driver a fiver in cash to augment his cell phone tip and checked the Alice B's façade. Above the main sign was a multicolored horizontal striped flag of the LGBTQ+ community and a smaller sign saying "Welcome to all peaceful folks." Inside was a long wooden bar, backlit with gaudy all-year Christmas lights and at the far end an open patio festooned with short trees and palm fronds. In the middle was a small stage for singers and small bands, facing a dance floor. The lunch crowd had gone and there were about ten people lounging in wicker chairs and a dozen more men and women on barstools. In one dark corner two women were making out.

I sat at the end of the bar and a tall, attractive dark-haired woman approached and flipped a coaster in front of me.

"What'll it be?" the bartender said. Yes, the deep voice tipped me off. Whichever gender she was born as, she was looking great now.

"House Chardonnay," I said. "Too late for lunch?"

"No way," she said, jerking her thumb at a menu tacked to the wall. "Kitchen's open 'til midnight."

"Hamburger medium and fries," I said.

She nodded and walked to the other end of the bar, where she shouted my order to a cook, then came back, placed a wine glass and poured a La Crema almost exactly to the rim. I figured I might need a straw to get it started.

"Great pour," I said. "You'll make someone a wonderful wife."

Laughing, "I already do," she said.

"Nice place," I said, looking around, purposely hoping I looked like a tourist.

"Thanks. First time here?"

I took a sip and nodded. "Yeah, just got to town. You the owner?"

"One of them. Three of us bought the place seven years ago." She brushed the hair off her shoulders and leaned back, looking me over.

I gave the owner a toasting gesture and took another sip. "Congratulations," I said.

"Where you from?"

"L.A. I'm actually looking for a long-lost friend who moved here a year ago. "Thought I'd start with a couple of saloons."

"What's his name?"

"A woman. Name's Cindy."

"Is she queer?"

What the hell, I thought. In for a penny, in for a pound. "You mean lesbian?"

I had already decided she'd made me out as a straight guy, but this apparently confirmed it.

She grinned, flashing beautiful teeth. "Yes," she said. "I mean lesbian." She stepped to the bar and offered a handshake. "I'm Patsy."

I shook hands. "Steve," I said. "Cindy and I worked together, but I lost touch when she moved."

"I don't know the name, but I'll ask around." Patsy turned and strolled along the bar to the far end, checking people for seconds. At the end she spoke to a few people then turned and spoke to the cook.

Two minutes later a woman appeared at my elbow and placed my hamburger plate on the bar. "Here you go," she said. "Burger medium with fries." She put the check on the bar and turned to go.

"Hold on," I said. "Do you happen to know a Chinese woman named Cindy?"

She shook her head. "It doesn't sound familiar, but I only work days. Maybe Patsy would know."

"Thanks. She's asking around." She nodded and walked away as I picked up the burger and munched. Not bad. The proper bread-to-meat ratio, for a change. You don't get it in most burger joints.

I finished the food and wine and flipped a twenty on the bar as Patsy came back. "Nope, no luck."

"Thanks anyway," I said as she made change for the twenty.

"There's a place up the street a few blocks called 'The Wild One.' You might try there." Patsy put three ones on the bar but I left them there.

"Thanks again," I said.

The façade of The Wild One looked like a Victorian house, brightly painted blue with white railings, balustrades and window trim. Inside it looked like a combination queer bar and dive hangout, a lot like the place I'd just come from. Instead of the stage and dance floor it had an amp and speaker area for guest bands and a turntable set-up for disk jockeys. There was a dartboard on a red velvet wall near one corner, and a red-felt pool table. Bright Christmas-like lights were everywhere and I wondered whether this was standard décor for queer bars, but I remembered that this was no longer considered a "queer bar."

The walls were almost totally covered by posters—mostly of old movies, "African Queen," "The Petrified Forest," "Key Largo," and the oldest one being "Casablanca." Now that I think about it, they were all Humphrey Bogart films. There were also porcelain head sculptures, banners, license plates, old political bumper stickers, corny artwork of almost nude fat women, and practically anything else one could imagine. One framed photograph showed Marlon Brando and Lee Marvin sitting on motorcycles and toasting each other with pitchers of beer. Behind the bar was a garden area with palm fronds and ferns climbing up trees and poles, with dirt flooring and various stuffed chairs and couches haphazardly arranged throughout. There had to be a kitchen somewhere, but I couldn't see one.

A Google search had told me the place had been in business since 1957, and was originally a strictly straight neighborhood bar named after the movie. When it became acceptable for the LGBTQ+ people to come out, two lesbians had bought it, kept the name except for a new connotation, and after a brief neighborhood resistance complete with graffiti and broken windows, had become accepted and now a popular bar and grill frequented by everyone throughout the Bernal Heights area of San Francisco.

I perched on a comfortable wicker stool with armrests and took it all in. There seemed to be a good crowd for mid-afternoon. The barstools were about three-quarter full, and most of a cluster of small dining tables were taken with either post-lunch loiterers or couples sharing a private drink.

A good-looking guy who looked like he was still in college came over and flipped a napkin/coaster in front of me—why do all bartenders do that? He had crew-cut blond hair, clean-shaven, and wore a white dress shirt and black trousers, with a military-type nameplate on the shirt that said "Ivan."

"Howdy," he said, "what'll you have?"

"Got any Johnnie Walker Blue?" I thought I'd switch to Lynch's fave to change my luck.

The kid laughed. "Mister, I've been here two years and you're the first customer *ever* to order that." He laughed again.

I smiled back at him. "Do I take that as a no?"

"Yes, no," he said. This was going to be fun.

"So, I don't suppose you'd have Johnnie Walker Green."

"There is such a thing?"

"Just kidding. I don't even know. I'll have the Red, with a water back."

"You got it," he said, and turned away.

I looked around more carefully but didn't see any Chinese women. Ivan returned with my drink and I took a quick sip.

"Can you help me?" I said. "The bartender down at Alice B's suggested I come here for some info." He nodded, as if it happened all the time. "I'm just up from L.A. and looking for a long-lost friend," I continued. "A Chinese woman named Cindy. And I thought I'd start with a few bars. Ever heard of her?"

He nodded and twisted his mouth as he looked up at the ceiling. "Don't know her personally, but there's a woman named Cindy comes in every day for a few drinks right after work."

"Oh? I hit the jackpot so fast?" I couldn't believe my luck.

"But she's not Asian," he said.

"Not Asian. Chinese," I said.

"Yes," he said. "And Chinese are Asian."

I couldn't help smiling. Here we go again, I thought. "Yeah, I know. But all Asians aren't Chinese. My Cindy is Chinese. Not Japanese, not Indian, not Vietnamese, not Korean. Chinese." I took another drink.

"Yes, yes," he said quickly, nodding as if talking to a six-year-old. "Let's start over. There's a Cindy comes in every night around five-thirty. But she's white."

"Why didn't you just say that?" He just looked at me and I could tell I was starting to piss him off, so I modulated my speech as best I could. I looked at my watch. "Thanks for the info. I'd like to talk to her, but what can I do to waste three hours around here?"

He shrugged his shoulders, visibly glad to have the subject changed. "Not much. There's a movie theater not far from here that features old classic movies. Where you staying?"

"Motel by Fisherman's Wharf," I lied.

"Oh, so you got a car?" When I nodded, he said, "So you could go hang out down there, or go to the Ferry Building and walk around there. Or you could take the ferry over to Sausalito and see that town. Kind of touristy, but the ferry might be fun for an LA guy."

"Thanks again," I said, throwing a ten on the bar. I had no interest in crisscrossing downtown again. "I think I'll try the movie. See you in a while."

"I'll be here," he said. "Careful about parking around there. Getting towed can ruin your day."

I took another Uber back to my car and I managed to find a handicapped zone a half-block from the movie house and hung a phony handicapped card Johnny Lynch had smuggled to me on my mirror. The movie house had two screens, each showing a favorite of mine: "The Man Who Shot Liberty Valance" and "Shane." I Googled each movie and saw that they totaled almost four hours, so I decided to watch the first part of "Valance" until my favorite line—when John Wayne says, "That's MY steak, Liberty…YOU pick it up!"— and then go over to watch all of "Shane." That should eat up the time and get me back to The Wild One soon after my target appeared.

Ivan waved at me as soon as I entered the saloon and by the time I approached him he had a Johnnie Walker Red waiting for me. He jerked his head to the right.

"She's down at the other end, talking to the guy in the cowboy hat," he said.

I thanked him and, with my drink, walked down to the end of the bar. She was a good-looking woman, maybe 30, 35, tall, well-dressed, with a single long brunette braid down to the middle of her back. Definitely not Chinese. She was talking with a younger man with an un-trimmed beard, husky build, cowboy shirt to go with his hat. He looked like he'd just stepped out of one of the movies I'd just seen.

"Excuse me," I said as I tapped her on the shoulder. "Pardon the interruption, but is your name Cindy?"

She turned, surprised, and smiled. Very attractive. The cowboy, however, was not pleased. A split second after she'd said "Yes?" he turned fully around to face me.

"Hey, pardner, we're having a conversation here," he said. Yes, he actually said "pardner."

"Yes, I know," I said, "and it's important that I talk to your friend here for just a few minutes, if you don't mind." I gave him the most sugary smile I could muster.

Meanwhile, Cindy had turned full face as well, and said, "Who are you?"

"Yeah, who are you?" cowboy said.

Totally ignoring him, I said to the woman, "I'm a private investigator and I'm looking for a certain woman who fits your description." It was just bait, I knew. But just maybe...I flashed my ID, carefully to show her and shielding it from the cowboy.

"Just a few minutes?" I said.

"Lemme see that," cowboy said, trying to step between us and grabbing at my ID folder.

She put her arm between us. "It's okay, Tony. Let me talk."

But he pressed on. "It's not okay. Lemme see that ID."

Now it was my turn. I made a big show of putting my folder back in my breast pocket and pushed his arm away. I stepped up close to his face and patted my chest, then held my arms back in a "surrender" gesture. "You'll have to take it back out yourself, pal," I said, looking up through his beard. "If you can read, that is."

He blinked at me, somewhere between complete surprise and disbelief. I think he was debating whether to take a swing at someone twice his age. I sort of hoped he would.

"Stop!" the woman said. Then, to cowboy, "Back off. Drink your beer."

He kept snarling and I didn't take my stare far from directly into his eyeballs. She tugged my arm and indicated an available table over by a wall under a velvet painting of a tiger.

"Okay, what's this about?" she asked.

"Sorry for the fuss there," I said, politely nodding toward her cowboy friend. "I'm looking for a woman who might be involved in a crime whose name is Cindy, and I've been asking around. Ivan over there said you were the only one around with that name."

"So?" she said. "What crime? What do you want to know?"

"Sorry," I said, "but the Cindy I'm looking for is Chinese. I just thought you might have heard about someone with the same name as you."

"Oh. Well, sorry. I think I'm the only one around here. But if I meet a Chinese Cindy, or hear of one, I'll let you know."

I nodded an apology and handed her my card. "Thanks for your attention, anyway," I said. "I appreciate your help." Then, "By the way, where do you work?"

"I'm a nurse," she said.

CHAPTER THIRTY-ONE

Game days—and game nights—in the city reminded MaryLou a lot of game days back home. Both had hordes of fans all dressed in the same-colored jerseys determinedly marching toward a shared destination in a rehearsed shuffle, advancing only as fast as the group in front would allow.

However, the high school games in northern Louisiana and the college games in Baton Rouge attracted some of the same people who might frequent a 24/7 Bass Pro Shop. But the fans of the San Francisco Giants appeared to be walking right out of a Land's End catalog, many with brand new gear and never-before-worn hats—extra lame for those with tags still on them. In a city of transplants, the new fans seemed to be edging out the die-hard locals without the same cash flow.

MaryLou couldn't complain though—she too was a transplant, although she could have fooled anyone by the way she was able to ride BART into the city and then switch to Muni without having to ask where the transfer stations were.

MaryLou was meeting Cassius for a game against the Rockies of Colorado. She was excited to see him; ever since he showed up at the wedding—and later apologized—they seemed to be getting back to the way things were in college. She was glad when he called to renew his long-time offer to take her to a game and teach her baseball. However, it *did* occur to her that dinner and a night game seemed a little odd instead of lunch and a day game. She remembered that Cassius knew damn well that her husband Walter worked nights.

MaryLou got off at the King St. & 2nd station and walked along the Embarcadero toward the Java house, an old, small wooden coffee house right on the bay off of pier 40. Here, the food was a fan favorite before the games, mostly due to the vastly cheaper prices between inside the ballpark and just outside the gates than any particularly spectacular dishes. Their hot dog does pair well with an Anchor Steam beer, though.

MaryLou stepped inside and removed her shades. Although it was a typical overcast August evening in the Bay Area, the last light refracting off all the micro-sized water droplets suspended in the air actually made it brighter than it would be on a clearer pre-game evening. As her eyes adjusted to the dim tavern, she scanned the interior, not seeing anyone in particular. Then, as she made her second pass with her eyes, she clocked Cassius walking out of the restroom toward an empty table. She approached and started giggling.

"I see you still have your Tulane gear," she said. "But why would you wear green to a Giant's game?" That much she'd learned: the Giants were an orange and black team.

He beamed at her. "I mean, I'm not going to buy a jersey for a team I don't even root for."

They embraced, MaryLou careful not to push against him too hard, he trying to hug a little too tightly. After the usual pleasantries exchanged between friends and MaryLou declining an offer for a beer or hotdog twice, they headed out toward Oracle Park.

This wasn't MaryLou's first time to Oracle Park, but it was her first time there for a baseball game. She had been to some monster truck rally there a few months ago. Not her idea, obviously it was Walter's, but she went anyway.

But now, at a ball game, the true majesty of the most beautiful park in the big leagues demanded her attention. The brick encircled the field and the amber of the walls balanced the orange of the fans making the entire stadium feel alive. Built around the turn of the millennium, the park is the crown jewel of the China Basin area of San Francisco.

MaryLou and Cassius were sitting in right field, on Levi's Landing. Behind her was an armada of kayakers, booze cruisers, and small sailboats patrolling the harbor, waiting for the crack of a home run to launch a souvenir to one lucky vessel. MaryLou made a mental note to join the McCovey Cove tradition one day. She knew a few doctors who had boats.

"So the Rockies bat first," Cassius explained, "because they're the visiting team."

MaryLou forgot the ruse for them to hang out tonight was for Cassius to *teach* her the game's rules. "Oh," she feigned interest. "So that means the Giants are in the field. So, who's pitching today?"

"One of our older arms, Johnny Cueto."

"Arms?

"That's what we call pitchers."

"Gotcha. So, what's new with you these days? How's work or whatever?" she asked, desperate to not be stuck talking about baseball for the next two hours—or three, or four. Apparently, no one knows when the game is going to end.

"It's going well, actually." He sounded surprised. "Got a raise, which is always nice, and the semiconductor business is thriving."

"I won't ask what a semiconductor is, but glad to hear it. What about non-work things? Seeing anyone recently?"

Cassius flinched. She knew he hated these questions, especially from her. But they both knew it was her tacit way of signaling that nothing was going to happen between them. Anything to show him she has moved on since, apparently, the wedding was not convincing enough.

"On and off. More off than on, really. Tried one of those dating apps everyone here seems to do."

"Everyone but me," she interjected.

"Yes, well we don't all have the privilege of being married to our soulmate now do we?" His words were both sarcastic and cutting. She ignored it.

"Anyway," he continued, "yeah, you know, been going on some dates, but the people here are nothing like the girls I would talk to growing up. You can't even mention that I own a hunting rifle and shotgun without needing to attend a five-hour lecture on how gun owners are just a cut above Satan. All while these dates puff their e-cigarettes marketed to kids, play on their cell phones probably made in sweatshops, and wear shoes poor kids might've stitched some place in southeast Asia making five dollars a month. It's frustrating."

"Wow, you really had to get that off your chest," MaryLou replied. "But that's California, I'm discovering."

Before Cassius could respond the crowd erupted. With a runner on second, the Giants pitcher had thrown a hanging slider over the plate that the Rockies shortstop had belted into triples alley—a part of the ballpark in center field notorious for stretching doubles into triples. However, the Giants centerfielder caught up to the ball on the fly and fired it back to second base on one hop, doubling up the runner between second and third before he could get back safely.

"You don't see that every day," Cassius said. "Caught him changing his mind."

"How do you know that?" she said.

"Well, he ran past second like he was going to third, but stopped and tried to get back. Decided he couldn't make it, but the throw got him. You don't see that every day."

"I certainly don't!" MaryLou replied with a wide grin.

The game ended only two hours later after a slick double play—a short game by baseball standards. The Giants had rallied in the seventh to go ahead by two and quickly retired the final six Rockies to get the win. Cassius and MaryLou were now getting out of the Uber they had ordered out of the stadium—a mistake in hindsight, since it seemed like everyone had the same idea. But after battling traffic, they were dropped off in Chinatown for some late-night dim-sum one of her nurse friends had raved about.

They stepped out into the crisp night air, even though it was August, when the marine air cools rapidly, turning summer to autumn almost daily. Thankfully MaryLou had lived here long enough to be prepared, and was bundled with the tried and true SF wardrobe of windbreakers, sweaters, and flannel. Cassius, however, was not as careful, but tried to tough it out to "impress" his date by not complaining about the cold. To his credit though, the restaurant was up a steep stairway and once they arrived, they both had built up a light sweat, requiring MaryLou to remove a few of her layers.

"Welcome," the hostess said, though not necessarily pronounced that way.

"Table for two, please." Cassius took the lead.

They were shown their table, toward the back adjacent to the rear exit onto a fire escape.

"Thank you," MaryLou said to their server. "And can I get some water please?"

"Sure, I'll tell your waiter. Any other drinks while I'm here? Tsingtao, baijiu?"

When MaryLou looked confused, Cassius said, "Tsingtao is a Chinese beer, pretty harmless, and baijiu is more like clear Chinese whiskey, only weaker."

MaryLou's eyes rolled and she said, "I think I'll stick with water."

"I think a nightcap sounds good," Cassius said. "I'll take some plum wine if you have any. Chilled."

"OK, one mijiu coming up, and for you?" she turned to MaryLou.

Shaking her head, "Not for me please. I'm set with just the water."

"Come on," Cassius pleaded, "let's drink like we used to in Caddo, like when we would sneak swishers and hurricanes out of that corner store."

"Nope, I think I'm OK never doing that again."

The server left them, with Cassius feeling dejected.

❧   ❧   ❧

The dinner was great. Whoever had recommended the place was spot on, the bao and potstickers were perfectly steamed and even the tea was somehow better than tea at home. But the conversation was slightly strained. MaryLou understood perfectly well what Cassius was hoping for, so she kept steering the conversation away from the "good old days" in Caddo and then college.

After their meal, which included more than a few cups of Chinese whiskey for Cassius, MaryLou asked for the check while he was in the restroom and paid in cash. She didn't want to use her credit card because she'd told Walter that she was having dinner in Palo Alto with a nurse friend.

When Cassius returned, he frowned at her. "What, you already paid?"

"Yeah, I need to get back home soon."

"Why? C'mon, have a nightcap. How about dessert?"

"No, this has been fun, Cassius, but I think it's time I get going. Might be hard to get back home if I stay out too late."

"I was planning on driving you home. I'd like to show you my place."

She shook her head. "No, Walter sometimes comes home early and I wouldn't want him to see you dropping me off."

"Well, shit." Now he was getting angry. "What the hell happened to us?"

"What do you mean? I thought today was a nice day of catching up with an old friend."

"You know what I mean." He was drunker than she thought. "I thought we had this deal. We made it out of that shitty town together, it's not supposed to be like this."

She got up to leave. He followed her, trying to calm down.

"I still love you, MaryLou. I always will."

"I'm married now, Cash. Doesn't that mean anything to you? I'm sorry about whatever false impression you had for tonight, but you have to stop thinking that way." Her Uber was two minutes out. Hurry up Griselda.

"There you go again. I thought we both had this unspoken agreement. We made it out together, and now you're treating me like someone you only *used* to know."

"There was no such 'unspoken agreement'," she said. "You have to get over this, Cash."

Her car was pulling up, but she had to cross the street. He reached out and grabbed her arm forcefully before she could get in the car. He tried to kiss her but she turned away. He stared at her with a look of contempt she hadn't seen since her father attended her high school graduation.

He let her go after a few extra beats. "And I could've paid for the fucking dinner. I probably make three times as much as you."

MaryLou got in the car and sped off. She was flustered and nervous. Then her phone buzzed.

"Text message from Walter."

Suddenly she wasn't looking forward to getting home.

CHAPTER THIRTY-TWO

Cassius awoke much the same way he did every Monday morning, in a panic. As he jolted out of bed, the bright rays of sunlight pouring into his loft reminding him he was late again, he tripped on his flight to the shower over the shoes he had taken off just a few hours ago.

Standing under the hot water, he cursed at himself for still being unable to properly start his day in a more mild-mannered routine. Chuckling to himself, he seemed to accept this is just who he was as a person, five minutes late to be considered early.

Choking down his usual cold Pop-Tart and sliding on his loafers, Cassius raced out the door to begin another week at his job. He had no joy in the engineering work he did, but the salary had made him accustomed to a lifestyle he never had growing up—weekends on his boat at Lake Berryessa in Napa Valley, Sunday brunches at the Coyote Point Yacht Club in San Mateo, and the occasional trips to Vegas for all-night blackjack at the Bellagio. Just the run of the mill activities for another engineer in Silicon Valley.

On his way down to the garage, Cassius passed an older man in the elevator. He wasn't anyone he had seen in his building before, which was unusual, but he was far too late to think twice about it. He unlocked his red BMW and started his commute south, down the Peninsula towards the south bay and the tech capital of the world.

Traffic wasn't that bad this morning. Cassius even made up some time as he raced down the 280 Freeway to work. He exited off his usual

Sand Hill Road stop and cruised east towards Palo Alto. Seeing that he wasn't as late as when he had started off, he pulled over at a new high-end coffee roastery at the Stanford Shopping Center and strolled in.

Although his employer provided fresh coffee daily, on top of massages, three-course lunches and dinners, and a full access gym, buying things outside of work was yet another extravagance Cassius had become used to.

Standing in line, he couldn't get over the fact that he was being watched. He stared down at his phone, trying to avoid eye contact with anyone. After checking his email for the third time in two minutes, he was convinced a pair of eyes were still on him. He glanced up and scanned the room. He saw many others just like him, similar age, similar dress, and similarly staring down at their glowing hands. He clocked the room and locked eyes with a much older man, clearly out of place in a Palo Alto coffee roastery. He had white hair and was wearing a tie, also quite strange for any Silicon Valley coffee house at this time of the morning.

Cassius blinked.

It was the same man he had passed on the elevator.

Before he could do anything, the barista asked him for his order. Automatically he regurgitated his usual coffee order— Grande Ethiopian blend with room for cream and a dash of cinnamon—and paid his bill. As he shuffled to the left toward the other waiting patrons, he looked around again, trying to find his tail, but it seemed the man had ducked out once he was spotted.

After Cassius retrieved his coffee from the counter and added the perfect chemical proportions of milk and cream, he stepped outside to finish his commute to work. However, before he could do that, leaning against the hood of his car was that same older man, staring directly at him.

"What gives, man?" he asked the stranger. "If I can help you just say so. Stop following me around."

"You're Cassius, right? Cassius Lemoor?" Steve Lombardi asked bluntly.

"Yeah, but I'm sure you knew that. You wouldn't just be tailing some stranger, would you?"

Steve smiled a little to himself. "Cassius from Mooringsport?"

"OK guy, now I'm really annoyed. What's the deal? I gotta get to work."

"I'm afraid you'll need to be a little late today," the old man retorted. "I need to talk to you about your friend, MaryLou."

Now he had Cassius' full attention. "Oh? What's going on?"

He was intentionally blunt. "She's dead."

Cassius looked at him. "What the fuck are you talking about!"

"I'm sorry," Steve said. "She was found in McCovey Cove, apparently drowned."

"Are you shitting me? When?"

"A week ago," Steve said. "It's true. I'm sorry."

"It just can't be," Cassius said, shaking his head. "She could swim like a barracuda."

Steve caught him as Cassius suddenly sagged and reached out to grab a street sign.

"My god! Are you sure?"

"Sadly, yes. My name is Steve Lombardi." He flashed a credential card, some sort of license, but too quickly for Cassius to read. "Can I ask you a few questions?"

Cassius and Steve headed back into the coffee shop. They found a quiet corner at the end of a long communal table; however, the other occupants were typing away on their laptops with bulky headphones on. As private as you can get in public Silicon Valley.

"So, what are you, investigating her death or something?"

"Or something," Steve replied. An annoying answer to Cassius. "I'm a retired cop, just a P.I. now. But there were some background questions a few cop buddies asked me to look into."

"Our police are too busy to handle their own murder investigations now?" Cassius said under his breath.

"Murder...interesting." Steve snapped back. "What makes you say that?"

"Oh, don't give me that whole 'Gotcha, I caught you in a trap' routine. I had no idea she was dead until now. You wouldn't be here if she died in a car accident. Actually, I want to go call Ethan right now."

"You can do that in a second. I do need you to tell me a few things first."

"How did she die? Can't you see I'm in shock?" Now Cassius was getting angry.

"Fine, but you need to calm down, kid. She was stabbed and thrown into the bay."

"Stabbed? Holy Shit! By who?"

"As I said, I'm a P.I. Why do you think I'm here?"

"You think *I* did it?"

"I think you need an alibi."

"Is this where I say I need a lawyer?"

"So, tell me, when did you move out here from Texas?"

"How did you know I lived in—never mind. I've been here a while now. Two years, I guess. After a few years with a firm in Austin."

"And did you see MaryLou often? Did you move out here because of her?"

"No," Cassius said. He was getting irritated. "There's this place called Silicon Valley, in case you never heard of it. They recruit a lot of bright guys from other companies. The work brought me here, to a company in Sunnyvale. And yeah, I see MaryLou from time to time." He caught himself. "Saw."

"So, would you say you were friends?"

"Of course. We go way back to grammar school. I just went to dinner and a Giants game with her a while ago."

Steve perked up when he mentioned the Giants game.

"The Giants huh? Baseball fan? Where did you sit?"

"Kinda yeah, I guess I am now. Well, more so earlier this decade when they were good. We had good seats, in the first row in upper right field."

Right above McCovey Cove, Steve noted.

"Did you know she was married?"

"Yeah, but married friends can go out to a ball game, can't they?"

"So, if you were such good friends, why weren't you invited to her wedding?"

"What?"

Steve continued, "I heard there was a fight between you two at her wedding."

"Who told you that?"

"And I heard the fight was about who she married. Is that true?"

Now Cassius stood up. "No, it's not true. And it's none of your business. I'm done with this. I don't know who you are but I don't need this after the news you just told me."

Cassius turned to leave. By now the entire table was looking at them.

Steve chased him out. On the sidewalk he called out, "That's fine, but do you at least know where her father is? We can't find him in Louisiana."

That news made Cassius stop in his tracks. He whipped around and marched right back to Steve.

"What do you mean, you can't find him?"

"I mean exactly what I said." Steve replied calmly. "The local rangers went to his property and he was gone, his truck was gone, and it looked like he hadn't been there for some time."

"Oh, God." Cassius felt the blood pool in his feet.

"My thoughts exactly. So, you think you can give me a hand, seeing as we know who we're dealing with?"

"That son of a bitch." Cassius looked around now, paranoid. "Do you think he's here?"

"We don't know where he is, that's what I'm telling you. But it is strange that he is gone and MaryLou turns up dead. We in the business call that suspicious."

Cassius looked down at Steve. "You really need to work on your empathy."

"I'll work on that tomorrow. Today, I'm working on this."

"Well, I haven't seen that asshole since the high school prom. I couldn't tell you where to look. However, Ethan, MaryLou's brother, might. He lives in Santa Rosa now."

Steve began taking notes. "Why do you think he'd know?"

"He stayed in touch with MaryLou when he was in the service. Pretty much the only thing Hiram liked about his kids was that his son was in the Navy."

"I heard they severed all contact with the father."

"Yeah, they did. But some of my friends back home told me Hiram bragged about Ethan in the local bars."

"Good to know." Steve glanced at his watch. "I got to run, but don't go far. Don't want to have to find you, too."

Cassius didn't say anything, just walked to his Beemer, jumped in and squealed away. Steve noticed that he sped off north, however.

Sunnyvale was to the south.

CHAPTER THIRTY-THREE

I have heard, but never experienced, that every once in a great while the very thing a P.I. is searching for, and is about to give up on, falls right into his lap.

That happened to me in my search for MaryLou Kowalski's killer.

I had had a long and wet lunch with Johnny Lynch at Liverpool Lil's, with nothing much to talk about but the paltry progress we'd been making. No new developments, no new evidence turning up, and the pressure building at City Hall to begin an official investigation into Johnny's culpability in the murder.

In short, we both knew it wouldn't be much longer before they arrested him for murder one. And it would make all the papers, big time.

At three o'clock or so we called it a day and agreed to try and get together with Bill Ralston in the morning to weigh our options. We shared the bill and staggered only mildly to our cars. I had to laugh about the bill. It was a hundred and twenty-two dollars. We'd each had a hamburger. I recalled one-time Johnny was in uniform and we had lunch one day when he was on his way to work and because we weren't drinking, the bill was twenty-seven bucks! Now, in my mellow mood, I tried to subtract twenty-seven bucks from a hundred and twenty-two. I decided that it was a serious health hazard for an Irish cop and an Italian former cop to dine together when they were off duty!

Besides, the Giants were in New York for a night game series with the Mets and I wanted to catch the game on TV at four o'clock.

The fog across the bridge required intermittent windshield wipers, and I slipped an Errol Garner CD into the slot and carefully stayed in the right lane. I'm not proud of the fact that every now and then—not often, mind you— there suddenly would appear two center stripes on the bridge and I have to hold one hand over an eye to make them one.

I know, I know. You'd think I would know better.

I took the first Mill Valley turnoff, went slowly up Miller Ave. and turned left at the 2 A.M Club. My car, like the old horses that pulled milk wagons, knew the way and wanted to park at the Club but I managed to fight it off and made it up the hill to my driveway, and up the driveway to my garage.

The first thing I did was start a pot of coffee on the stove, which would go well with a nice glass of my four-dollar swill during the game. I changed into sweat pants, a T-shirt, and slippers and sat back to enjoy the Giants losing again.

San Francisco is a great city in which to be a baseball fan. Three World Series in five years, a beautiful downtown park, ferry boat access to it, and what some of the strangest cast of characters will do to a ballpark crowd! However, I keep hearing that young people don't like the sport anymore. Basketball is quickly overtaking baseball, and for the life of me I don't know why. I hear all the arguments many make about why baseball is boring—the pace of play, the length of the season, the game stoppages—but all those same arguments apply to basketball.

Basketball is forty-eight minutes of the exact same thing, a dunk, a shot, a steal, or a miss. Is what these athletes are doing really that compelling if the final score is 115-114? The last two minutes or so are the only times of real excitement, and they take the length of a quarter themselves with all the timeouts—similar to pitching changes.

Besides never seeing anything new during a basketball game, the people I talk to speak of the sport like a video game, where the off-season and players' personal lives are better than watching the games themselves. That's not a sport. Baseball playoffs are entertaining because they are high leverage every time, and short. Same with March madness. That means the sports themselves aren't boring, the seasons are just too long.

I thought all of this about basketball until November 2015, that's when the Warriors "happened." Much like I thought my old friend Johnny Lynch was a boy scout who would spontaneously combust if he ever even thought about breaking any rules, and now here we are three Larry O'Brien Trophies and an affair later. Funny how things change.

Anyway, I was sitting in my sweatpants staring at the baseball diamond glow through my TV, Kruk and Kuip filling the silence of my living room. It wasn't long before I was screaming at Bruce Bochy to bunt, goddamit, BUNT! He drove me crazy. Giants were tied 1-1, and in the top of the third their first man up singled and the next guy walked. So, first and second, nobody out, score tied. I maintain every Little League player on the continent knows in that situation the next hitter—unless he's Babe Ruth or Barry Bonds—must *bunt*! Give up an out and get your two guys to second and third, right? But no. Bochy's favorite strategy seems to be hitting into a double play!

Anyway, Bochy doesn't bunt, double play, two out, man on third, the next guy pops out. Almost drives me to drink.

Which is what I was starting to do again in the eighth inning, when the same situation came up. Two on, nobody out, score tied this time at 5-5. Brandon Belt up, lefty yet. Bunt, of course.

It was when I started screaming that the phone rang. One ring, Belt swings and misses. Goddamit! Second, ring, Belt swings and misses again. Third ring, grounder into a double play.

When I reached for the phone it was to throw it into the TV screen, but I decided to talk into it first.

"Hello?"

A female voice said, "You seem out of breath."

"I was shouting at Bruce Bochy. Who is this?"

"Your card doesn't have an address." The voice was soft, slow, like an FM radio jockey.

"I'm particular about who visits me. Who is this?"

"You said that."

"You didn't answer it."

"It's important that I meet with you. Where do you live?"

She had a slightly southern accent. "Are you selling vacuum cleaners?"

"Mr. Lombardi, this is serious stuff. I want to meet you."

"Where are you, whoever you are? I'm in Mill Valley. Several nice bars."

"Too noisy," she said. "It's Happy Hour. We need privacy."

I had to laugh. "Oh, so *that's* what you're selling. I have to compliment you on your innovative marketing strategy."

I thought I heard a chuckle. "Wrong again."

"Tupperware?" I said. "Wounded Warriors?"

An audible sigh. "What is your address? I can be in Mill Valley in twenty minutes."

"I have to know who you are. It's part of my business plan."

"I'm someone you want to meet. I guarantee it."

"How did you get my phone number?"

"It's on your card, silly." A girlish chuckle.

"Yes, silly me. Where did you get my card?"

"That's part of why you need to meet me. Mr. Lombardi, I've just turned onto 101 in San Rafael. Now I can be there in fifteen minutes. Give me a knocking code or a ring sequence." A pause. Then, "So you'll know I'm not selling pots and pans."

Now it was me who paused. I tried to discern an accent, but no. A regional patois, maybe Louisiana? No again.

I said, "Let's play a game while you drive. You have a southern accent. Where are you from?"

"Tampa."

"Did you go to school there?"

"Brooks Debartolo Collegiate High School."

I raised my eyebrows. "Sounds fancy."

"Very exclusive. My parents were wealthy."

"What college did you go to?"

"No college, per se. My grades were so fabulous I went directly into medical school."

"You're a doc?"

"Yes, you're getting warm. And I'm turning off onto Blithedale Avenue."

I was getting it. Also becoming extremely interested in this call. "So, don't tell me. I'll take 'Hospitals' for a thousand, Alex."

"You may be the next champion."

"San Francisco General."

"Bingo. I'm an ophthalmologist there."

"Turn left at the light with Chase Bank on the corner. Then right onto Miller at the high school. Right at the stop sign, 2 A.M. Club on the left. Up the hill, keep bearing right. One two seven seven Skyline. All the way up the driveway."

She hung up abruptly.

This was going to be one helluva meeting.

In exactly eight minutes my doorbell rang.

I had gone to the bathroom to comb my hair, touch up a few things, gargle to maybe get the old scotch out of my breath, and took a quick leak so as not to interrupt whatever conversation was about to ensue. I threw a few sofa pillows around to spiffy up the living room, stacked the magazines on the coffee table a little neater, removed a few glasses from the kitchen sink to the dishwasher, and threw on a Notre Dame sweatshirt over my T-shirt.

Then I got my Ruger out of its shoulder holster in the bedroom, put it deep into my sweat pants, and went to the door.

When I opened it, I thought I had been miraculously transported back to a Hawaiian resort with the hula girls giving out leis to the weary tourists. To say she was gorgeous would be like saying the sky was blue. She was short, shapely, nicely coifed jet-black hair, make-up as if she'd been to modeling school. She wore a conserva-tive-length dark blue skirt, and wide white belt and a white blouse under a baby-blue cardigan sweater.

And she was Chinese.

She put out a tiny hand. "How do you do, Mr. Lombardi. I'm Cindy."

CHAPTER THIRTY-FOUR

Well. Another punch in the *la bonza*. Or maybe just the mountain coming to Mohammed.

I think I just stood there, blinking for a few moments. Then I took her dainty hand and shook it slowly. I said something totally dumb, like, "You have no idea how glad I am to meet you."

She held her smile. "Oh, yes I do," she said. "May I come in?"

I felt foolish. "Uh, yes, of course," I said, ushering her past me into the living room. "Please sit down."

Which she did, tugging her skirt down, knees together, and put her purse on the cushion next to her, then clasped her hands together.

"Can I get you anything?" I asked. "Coffee? Tea? A drink, maybe?"

"Nothing, thank you. Maybe just water."

"Coming up. Er ... do you mind if I have a drink? This is something of a shock."

"I'll bet it is," she said, shaking her head.

I went into the kitchen and got her a small bottle of Perrier and a glass, then made myself a scotch-and-soda. Weak on the scotch—I was still slightly tipsy from the lunch with Johnny and I didn't want to miss any important information during the conversation that was about to begin.

Back in the living room I gave her the Perrier and drew up a chair in front of the coffee table.

I lifted my glass in a toast. "To repeat, I'm awfully glad to meet you."

She lifted her glass. Just nodded.

"Have you been to the police? I'm guessing no."

She shook her head. "A bartender introduced me to someone who said you were looking for me and gave me your card."

"You realize I have to give your name to an Inspector Ralston, who's heading up the investigation. You're considered a suspect in the murder of MaryLou Kowalski."

She lowered her eyes and reached over and pulled a tissue out of her purse. "I thought as much," she said.

"Shall I start?" I asked. "I have a thousand questions."

She nodded. "I have the time, Mr. Lombardi. I'm here to answer them all."

"Well, let's start with blunt. Did you kill Marylou Kowalski?"

"No, I did not."

"Did you tattoo your name on her butt?"

"Yes, I did."

I tried a little humor to loosen things up. "You have to quit stalling around and give me direct answers."

It seemed to work. She laughed. I shook my head and took a sip. "Okay, Doctor … er … hey, what is your last name?"

"Liang. But please call me Cindy."

"Okay, Cindy. Let's start from the very beginning."

She nodded again, sipped her Perrier.

"How did you meet MaryLou?"

"It was quite coincidental," she said. "MaryLou went suddenly blind in one eye one evening while watching television. In her panic she called the hospital and got an emergency appointment with an ophthalmologist, which turned out to be me. The next morning, she could once again see out of that eye but she kept the appointment to find out what exactly had happened. I examined her and sure enough, there was nothing whatsoever wrong with her eye."

"So she just as suddenly could see perfectly?"

"Right. I pondered and pondered, and finally concluded that perhaps a bit of plaque had dislodged from an artery somewhere and came through her optic nerve instead of her brain. In other words, she had a stroke, but an optical one."

"Okay, I think I get it," I said. "So then what?"

"I quickly got her an appointment with a diagnostic sonographer, that is, an ultrasound technician, to check her carotid artery for blockage. And sure enough, she was ninety-five percent blocked."

"So hold on," I said. "Isn't she a bit young for that sort of condition? I mean, I thought only old guys like me got their arteries blocked. We're talking cholesterol, right?"

She nodded. "Right. But, again by sheer coincidence, I'd read a recent paper a cardiologist friend had sent me, which found that hidden thickening of the arteries—atherosclerosis—was more prevalent in young people than was conventionally thought. And it can be hereditary. It was written by a Canadian cardiologist."

"So then what?"

"Well, to make the long story short, she was sent directly to a vascular surgeon, who performed an emergency endarterectomy. Then she was fine. A few weeks later I got a note from her thanking me profusely for—she made air quotes— 'saving her life.' Although doctors don't go into my specialty to save lives, she claimed that I saved hers and wanted to take me to dinner."

I smiled. "Kismet."

She laughed. "Exactly. I fell in love with her at the North Beach Restaurant."

"And that began the relationship."

"Yes."

I leaned back and took another sip. "When did you find out about John Lynch?"

"She told me one evening after we'd made love. I wasn't exactly thrilled with the news."

"I guess not," I said.

"Well, she had a husband, was seeing another man, and now she was seeing me. Three people! I was extremely angry, to say the least."

"But not angry enough to kill her."

"Of course not." She paused, looked down again. "Well, I did give her an ultimatum. It was either them or me—she couldn't have both."

"How did she take that?"

"She said she was going to divorce the husband. She wouldn't commit to Inspector Lynch."

"And how did *you* take that?"

"All I can say is I wasn't happy."

"Tell me about the tattoo."

"She knew I was mad enough about the heart, so when I proposed that I have a share in … what?… the real estate?"

My turn to laugh. "I suppose that's as good a description as any," I said.

She smiled back. "So she agreed to let me add my name to his heart."

"You did it yourself?"

She nodded. "With some silver nitrate and a quill pen."

"I presume you had some pretty intimate discussions. Did she tell you anything about her husband?"

"Oh, yes," she nodded vigorously. "She once told me she thought she had a psychological problem, a low opinion of herself, blamed that on rushing into marriage so quickly."

"She didn't love Walter? Even at first?"

"Not at all. You know, 'looking for love in all the wrong places?' She said she detested him, especially after he started hitting her. She was planning to divorce him even before she met me."

I shook my head. "She certainly waited too long for that," I said. "Did she ever sound like she was afraid for her life? That he would kill her?"

Cindy shook her head slowly and dabbed at her nose with the tissue. "I don't know," she whispered. "However, as bad as Walter was and as much as she talked about hating to go home, she said she couldn't go back to Louisiana, either, to her father who sounded like he was more dangerous than Walter. At least on her psyche, not just her physical well-being."

I asked, "What *about* her father? Hiram."

"She told me all about him, how he treated her and her brother terribly after their mother died. They each got out of there as soon as they could. He didn't even come to her college graduation and she didn't invite him to her wedding."

"But he somehow knew she was married."

"Apparently."

"Her brother told me he was a real bigot."

"You spoke with Ethan?"

I nodded. "I'm speaking with everyone I can find."

"Did he tell you about the fight?"

I looked up from my drink. "Fight? What fight?"

"The father showed up at their door. She was at work, but he and Walter had words. I guess he threw a punch at him."

I shook my head. "My God! He's in town? Walter had a black eye when I went to see him, and I always thought maybe she gave it to him."

She managed a smile. "Probably would have been a good guess otherwise."

"She certainly had a lot of people angry with her. I've heard about the row with Cassius at the wedding."

"I don't think Cassius knew about me," she said. "At least, she never mentioned it."

"I also presume you heard about her death at the hospital. They've pretty much kept it out of the papers, with Lynch being a cop and all."

"Yes, although I couldn't acknowledge how I knew her. Other than the optical stroke, I mean. She was very well thought of."

I polished off the rest of my scotch and stood up. "Well, Cindy, I suppose I believe you, but *I* don't matter. You'll have to convince the police."

"I just thought I should speak with you first." She looked at her watch. "Well, if that's all..."

"Thank you for coming. I hope you still have my card. Please do call me if I can be of any help."

"And I hope I've cleared up a few things for you," she said as she gathered her purse and walked to the door. She extended her delicate hand again.

"Good evening," she said.

"Good evening Cindy," I said, but I actually wanted to throw her back on the couch and plant a long one on her. Must be drunker than I thought. I should write all this information down before I forget any details.

Instead I made myself a much stronger scotch-and-soda.

CHAPTER THIRTY-FIVE

I'm not sure why, but I decided to wait a day or two before calling Bill Ralston with the news about Cindy Liang. Maybe I just needed to chew over our conversation and make some evaluations myself. Would an apparently brilliant and highly regarded ophthalmologist be so forthcoming as Cindy was? So ... trusting?

When I finally did tell him, Ralston was as shocked as I had been, and equally impressed by the coincidence. If that's what it was—they say there is no such thing as a coincidence, so maybe hanging out at the once-lesbian saloon and passing my card to the Caucasian Cindy wasn't such a long shot after all.

"Man, are you kidding me?" was his first reaction.

"All things come to him who waits," was my clever retort. Then I told him in detail about our conversation and tried as hard as I could to describe her looks.

"Sounds more like a cover girl than an eye doctor," he said. "I'll drop by and see her right away. Did you get her phone number?"

"No, but San Francisco General shouldn't be hard to find. And I'm pretty convinced she's innocent. She was so upfront about her relationship. She just didn't seem like the vengeful type."

"And it sounds to me like she had too much to lose, a person with her apparent brains and position."

"Exactly what I thought."

"Listen, I got a call from Ethan Fitzgerald," he said. "He wants to set up some kind of funeral or memorial for his sister."

"That's strange. Who would come? We've been pretty good at keeping it all out of the papers. Not even an obit."

"I don't know," he said. "But I can't help him set it up, of course. I mean, while the case is still open."

"Think I should call him?"

"If you would. I'm not sure a funeral is a good idea."

"Why do you want me to call him if you think it's a bad idea?" I asked.

"I don't think we should get involved, but he also has no one to help him get in touch with all the people we have spoken to who knew his sister. Between the uninvited assistance and ability to track down people he's never met, just seems like a perfect job for a P.I. Maybe talk him out of it?"

"You laugh, but you'll be off the force one day too."

We mused a bit more about it. He rang off, then I called Ethan.

"Bill Ralston says you're thinking about a funeral," I said. "What's up? Do you think that's a good idea?"

"I just think we ought to do something," he said. "At least acknowledge her existence on earth, or whatever."

"Where are you thinking of doing it? In Mooringsport?"

"No, here," he said. "Nobody down there would give a shit."

"But who would you invite? It's been out of the papers, no obit..."

"I don't know. Listen, I'll be in town at the Ford dealer on Van Ness tomorrow. Can we get together?"

"Sure," I said. "Do you know Liverpool Lil's?"

"I've heard about it. How's two o'clock?"

"See you there."

Lil's had pretty much emptied out of the lunchtime crowd, and Ethan was sitting alone at the bar when I got there. After the usual greetings I ordered a drink.

"So," I said. "What are you thinking?"

"It just bothers the hell out of me that nobody's officially mourning her. Like, some kind of ceremony with prayers or something."

"Was she religious?"

"Not church-going religious, no. But she believed in God, and once told me she prayed to Him."

"But I can't help wondering who would you invite to such an event," I said. "Not too many people even know she's dead. Maybe a few friends and whoever did it."

He shrugged. "Let's think about that. Maybe you can help." He grabbed a napkin from behind the bar, clicked open a ballpoint pen, and started to write. "There's me and Cassius. She must have some friends at the hospital who know by now. I mean, who would come."

I nodded. "But Cassius is probably a suspect. Surely you can't invite suspects."

"Why not? All but one are innocent, right?"

He had me there. A sophistic puzzle? "You have a point. So ... maybe five or six at the hospital. She had a roommate, the gal she was hiding out with. Lucy."

"Yeah, that's what I mean about your help," he said. "I don't know any of those details about her personal life."

I nodded again. "And there's me and Lieutenant Ralston. She didn't know us, but now you and her husband do. And of course, her lover, my friend John Lynch."

"Hold on. Do you think *that's* a good idea?"

"That's what I'm talking about," I said. "He's the prime suspect. In fact, he may be arrested and charged any day now. Ethan, this is not a good idea!"

Ignoring me, he scribbled on the napkin. "What about her, um, other friend?"

"Yes, Cindy. She'd come, I'm sure," I said. "As far as anybody else knows, she's just her eye doctor."

"The husband?"

I just looked at him. He looked back at me and shrugged. "I'm supposing here," he said. "What do you think?"

I took a pull on my wine. "I don't know. He could cause a lot of trouble, from what I've heard."

"Let's make him a maybe. I wonder if he'd invite some of his own family."

"I doubt it."

"Who else?"

We both thought for a minute.

"Who we got so far?" I said finally, counting on my fingers. "Let's say five nurses, maybe a doc or two from the OR. You, me and John. Ralston. Cassius. Lucy and Cindy. What's that, fourteen? Fifteen?"

He looked at his napkin. "I've got fourteen. Not exactly a crowd."

"Ethan?"

He looked up. "Yeah?"

"Do you know your father's in town?"

He threw down his pen. "Bullshit!"

"It's true," I said.

"How do you know that?"

"Cindy told me. She said MaryLou told her that Hiram showed up at Kowalski's house. They had some kind of fight and he ran off. Then Kowalski's lawyer demanded a restraining order."

"Where the hell is he?"

I shook my head. "We don't know. They have an APB out on him now. Checking all the car rental agencies."

"Jesus," he said. "He's going to kill somebody!"

"Maybe he already has," I said.

He had started to write Hiram's name on the napkin but now scratched it off. "I don't believe it," he muttered.

"As I said, he, too, could cause a lot of trouble."

We said nothing for a long while, sipping our drinks. He looked at his watch and folded the napkin, tucked it in his pocket.

"I should beat the traffic," he said. "It's hellish getting past Petaluma."

"Don't I know it," I said. "But think about it. Also, where would you have it?"

"I don't know. I don't know the city at all. What do you advise?"

"Maybe some chapel somewhere? Maybe rent a small place, find a priest?"

"I just thought of something," he said. "What about a burial? Should I send her back to Mooringsport?"

I shrugged, picking up the bar tab and reaching for my wallet. "Your choice, I guess. It would be cheaper, that's for sure. Do you want me to check all this out for you? I'd be glad to."

"I'd sure appreciate it. Thanks for your help, Mr. Lombardi."

"Steve," I said. "I'll give you a call."

He got up and we shook hands. "I got the drinks," I said.

"Son of a bitch," he said, shaking his head and starting for the door. "The old bastard's here in town!"

Chapter Thirty-Six

I spent the rest of the day calling Ralston back to tell him about Ethan's plan, and took most of the next morning on the phone to research Ethan's idea for some kind of memorial ceremony.

Before I called Ethan with my results, I had lunch with Johnny to see what he thought. We chose Tarantino's on Fisherman's Wharf, mostly because neither of us had been there in more than ten years. Johnny used his police pass to park.

"Sounds a little dicey to me," is what he thought. "You got two guys in the same room who would like to see me dead."

"I'd say three," I said, nodding. "And at least two women." I couldn't help adding, "I'd say you're a regular All Star!"

To his credit, he did manage a smile. He took a drink and pushed his plate away. "I don't like it. What if they're all packing?"

"Ralston and I could take care of that. Besides, it's Ethan's wish. You don't have to attend."

He shook his head. "I wouldn't miss it for the world. I'll wear my vest."

I had to laugh. "Don't worry about it. I'll keep you out of the crossfire."

He smiled for the second time since we'd sat down. "Thanks a helluva lot."

The waiter cleared our plates, and carefully scraped the remaining sourdough bread crumbs from the tablecloth with his special tool, which I always suspected was a ritual performed in no other city in the nation.

"Any idea who else might be interested?" I asked.

"What about Ralston's partner, what's-his-name?"

"Keene. Nah, he never knew her."

"You sure Kowalski wouldn't bring some relatives?"

I shook my head. "Ethan told me they're a bunch of hicks who don't give a damn. Besides, he said MaryLou wouldn't want them there."

"I guess that's about it. Maybe Cassius has some friends who knew her."

"Not that well, apparently. I called him with the idea and he didn't think he'd bring anybody else."

"Well, that's it, then. When does he want to do it?"

"I'll ask him." I grinned again at him. "In any case, I'm sure your calendar's clear."

He made a fake gesture of throwing his drink in my face, but instead he downed it.

I did the same.

"Have a seat and open a beer," I said when Ethan answered his phone.

"You sure work fast," he said.

"That's because I'm not on the clock."

He laughed. "Just a second. I'll get the beer."

When he came back, he said, "Okay, I'm taking notes."

"I found there's a little chapel at the rear of Saints Peter and Paul Church on Washington Square. People can reserve it for what they call a 'donation,' and it's a good central location. And there's an old Italian priest who will say a few words."

"Great," he said.

"I've called Cassius and Cindy and they're on. I also called Lucy, who will let the hospital people know. And Bill Ralston, of course."

"Kowalski?"

"Still your call. I think he's dangerous."

"I've been thinking about that," he said. "What if we did it and he found out after the fact? He'd be really pissed off."

"There's another wrinkle that could calm him down a bit if you did invite him. No one has claimed the body from the coroner's office yet. Which probably means Kowalski doesn't want to be bothered. As the husband, he'd have the first claim priority. Maybe he's just too cheap. But whatever, you could call him as next of kin, her brother, and politely ask his permission to have her transported to Mooringsport where you have arranged for her to be interred in the local cemetery, next to her mother. Hanson & Sons Mortuary has agreed to handle it for about a third the price you'd pay here."

"Wow, you really did some homework, didn't you?"

"Kowalski would be hard put to turn that down. There's some paperwork involved, state permits for transport of the body and such, which he'll have to sign. But he should agree, and when he does, you can also politely invite him to the memorial you took the liberty of arranging."

"Okay, I'll do it," he said.

"You'll have to contact a mortuary here to pick up the body and prepare it, what's called a 'removal service.' And then call the mortuary in Mooringsport to confirm the arrangements and sign some more papers. Lots of bureaucratic bullshit."

"I'll do whatever's necessary."

"What an angel."

He laughed. "I guess I have to sell a lot of cars pretty soon."

"Or move up to Teslas," I said.

"So, let's see. Can you set it up for, say, this coming Saturday?"

"That's pretty quick, but probably. About three o'clock would be good."

"Okay, I'll call a local mortuary and arrange for them to deliver MaryLou and pick her up."

"Sounds good. I'll be in touch."

We clicked off and I poured another drink before I called the church.

And the invitees.

I decided it would be easier to park in Larkspur and enjoy a brief ferry ride across the bay, just in case Johnny and I got together after the sure-to-be sad memorial service and downed a few adult beverages. So, I dusted off my Clipper card to take that scenic route, assuming I still had some funds on my card to pay for the ride. And I could take an Uber back to my car in Marin.

On the drive to the ferry I noticed the old fighter pilots were out with their drones, but were all huddled on the ground instead of flying them. Was something wrong? I stopped and got out to watch. They then spread out, launched their drones and flew them in formation far out over the small bay inlet that bordered the park. Then, as I looked up at the squadron of drones coming back at us at about a thousand feet in the air, I suddenly had a chill. One formation slot was empty—it was a "missing man" formation, the traditional military tribute to a pilot who had passed away or been shot down. I figured it was probably one of the vets I had been watching on my runs.

In my mind I imagined it was for MaryLou—was it a coincidence I was heading for her memorial service?

I budgeted about two hours to arrive, door-to-door. Or door-to-church. The ferry from Marin to the Ferry Building on the San Francisco Embarcadero waterfront is spectacular. There's no better way to see the skyline, the Golden Gate Bridge in the distance, plus Angel Island and Alcatraz, than from the water. We even passed close by San Quentin Prison on the left soon after launch, and I couldn't help wondering if my old buddy John Lynch would be taking up residence there soon.

I sat outside on the back upper deck, enjoying the occasional sprays of mist and ignoring the diesel fumes. We docked at the Ferry Building and I walked across the busy intersection towards the Embarcadero plaza and the cable car stop. I caught the next car just as I arrived, and rode on the outside running board the whole way, which it seemed like I hadn't done since I was a teenager. I transferred on Powell Street, rode down to Columbus and jaywalked toward the twin-spired church across Washington Square. I remembered it was not only the church in which Joe DiMaggio married Marilyn Monroe, but also the church with the spires off which Quasimodo Charles Laughton, as the Hunchback of Notre Dame, poured boiling oil on the riotous mob below in 1939.

Ethan was outside with Ralston, sharing a few drags of a cigarette. Ralston dropped the butt and extinguished it with a quick pivot of his boot as I approached.

"You made it," Ralston said, for no apparent reason.

I turned to him. "So how's it looking in there?"

"Awkward. I had to come out here for a smoke just to break the tension."

"Did you frisk them?"

Ralston laughed and nodded. "Two .22 pistols and a MACE sprayer. What a world."

"Yeah. Johnny inside?"

"No, he was waiting for you, to go in together. He's in the nave of the main church. Go get him."

I did. He was way down in front, in the second pew, looking reverently up at the crucifix as he prayed. I knelt next to him.

"Ready for this?"

He was surprised to see me. Probably because the inside of a church was not one of our normal meeting places.

"I'm still not sure this is a good idea," he said.

I noticed he had his vest on, and patted his chest. "Expecting fireworks?"

"Can't be too careful," he said. He folded his rosary beads into a palm and slipped them into a side pocket as he pushed himself up and joined me. We walked slowly up the center aisle, past kneeling Chinese, whites, Filipinos and Latinos, mainly middle- and old-aged women, offering gratitude, supplication or whatever other petitions they silently prayed for.

Outside, we strode in step behind Ralston toward the chapel. Once the door closed behind us it took me a second for my eyes to adjust to the dimmer lighting indoors. Then I saw what Ralston had been talking about. At the front of the room stood Ethan, adjusting a large portrait of MaryLou in full nurse uniform, probably a graduation photo, above the open casket as a Funeral Director arranged a few vases of flowers surrounding it. She looked beautiful. Her hair appeared redder than I'd seen it, but then again I had only seen her on the M.E.'s exam table.

Also at the front, speaking to Ethan, was Cassius. They were being watched intensely by Kowalski, who brooded in the front row, in the side-aisle chair by the wall, looking closer to fighting Cassius than mournful of his deceased wife.

I kept scanning and saw Cindy and Lucy chatting in hushed voices in the third row of fold-out chairs. In the fourth and fifth rows were unidentified nurses and a few somber men I took to be OR or ER docs—though they may be nurses themselves too so you never know. The cute doc was also there, the one who examined me and refused to put a steak on my face when I went in to ask about MaryLou.

Johnny stayed in the back row, while I went up to the front of the casket and made a show of blessing myself and kneeling down in prayer. I got up and shook hands with Cassius and Ethan, whispered to them how wonderful MaryLou looked and then, with a glance toward Kowalski, sat in the front row and turned and beckoned Lucy and Cindy to join me.

Which they did, as Cassius also joined us. The Italian priest sat in a chair next to the casket. The Funeral Director kept inconspicuous to the side.

Ethan then went to the stage and turned to face the group. He didn't need a microphone in the confined room.

"I want to thank you all for coming. I know this is a hard time for everyone in the room, and my sister has a special place in each and every one of your hearts. This is Father Vito Bertoldo, who has graciously agreed to say a few words for us. After Father blesses MaryLou for the final time, he'll close the casket and leave us to say a few words among ourselves in private. Father, please?"

Ethan sat down next to me and Cassius as Father Bertoldo rose and opened his little leather-bound book. Everyone stood.

"In the name of the Father...."

And almost everyone in the room made the Sign of the Cross. Out of the corner of my eye I watched Kowalski stand stiffly, immobile.

To my surprise, Father Bertoldo read several prayers in Latin, which, or course, no one understood, except for a few words remembered from grammar school or high school. I was certain Johnny Lynch and I were recalling the same phrases from our days at St. Ignatius High in San Francisco.

Father then switched to the Lord's Prayer, which *almost* everyone recited with him. Then he looked up and recited from memory.

"In your hands, O Lord, we humbly entrust our sister MaryLou. In this life you embraced her with your tender love; deliver her now from every evil and bid her eternal rest. The old order has passed away; welcome her into paradise, where there will be no sorrow, no weeping or pain, but fullness of peace and joy with your Son and the Holy Spirit forever and ever."

Most of us said, "Amen."

Then he picked up an aspergillum, the little vessel with a sprinkler in it, sprinkled holy water on MaryLou, and said, "Eternal rest grant unto her, O Lord." And a few of us said, "And let perpetual light shine upon her." Then he said, "And may her soul and all the souls of the faithful departed, through the mercy of God, rest in peace."

And a few of us again said, "Amen." Father then solemnly closed the casket, picked up his book and aspergillum and shook hands with Ethan, then quietly left the small stage.

The room was quiet for several minutes, probably so everyone could say their own private prayer. Ethan went back to the stage, turned to us and said, "I don't really have much to say. MaryLou and I grew up together in a small town in northern Louisiana, and we were very close in our young years. But after she went off to college and I joined the Navy, we didn't see much of each other, although we kept in touch. I always regretted not being closer in the past few years, but each knew we loved each other. I always respected how everyone she met simply adored her."

"Apparently not!" Kowalski suddenly shouted from the side wall. There was an audible gasp from the group of hospital friends in the center rows. While heads turned toward Kowalski, expecting more, Ethan never acknowledged him. Lucy held up her hand and Ethan motioned her up. She stood nervously and looked around the room and then directly at the hospital people.

"I'm Lucy Reynolds. I'm a nurse and had the great privilege to work with MaryLou from the first day I arrived at General. She took me under her wing, never once admonished me when I made a few horrible mistakes and almost killed people." She laughed and a few of the medical people joined her. "That was one of our private jokes. Suffice to say I loved her dearly and I'll miss her more than anything. I even let her move into my tiny apartment when … when …"

Lucy broke down in tears and Ethan escorted her off the stage. Back on, he looked around, avoiding Kowalski's glare. He looked directly at Cindy, who slowly shook her head "no" and dabbed at her eyes with Kleenex. She and Lucy embraced each other.

Ethan looked at Johnny Lynch but caught himself and looked down at me. I also shook my head, but in quiet agreement with Johnny's decision.

Then he looked down at Cassius, who got up and stepped onto the stage.

"I'm Cassius Lemoor and I went to high school with MaryLou back in Mooringsport." He looked around the room and I knew he was looking for Hiram Fitzgerald, who wasn't there.

"When we graduated, we went down to New Orleans together and went to separate colleges, but saw each other often. She even let me share her car."

A gentle chuckle from the room.

"And when we both graduated, she gave me a lift to Austin, where I had a job, and she was on her way to a job she got in San Francisco. That was the kind of girl she was."

Cassius held back a sob, paused, composed himself. "When I eventually moved to Silicon Valley we kept in touch."

He looked over at Kowalski with venom in his eyes. "*Very* close touch," he said evenly.

I flinched. He looked down at me and I gave him the theatrical "cut it" sign with the finger slash across my throat.

The kid got it. "That's all I have to say. She was the most fabulous woman I've ever known, and I'll be the luckiest man in the world if I ever meet someone like her again."

He left the stage weeping and covered his eyes with a handkerchief.

"Well then," Ethan said. "I thank you all again and I—"

"Hold on!"

It was Kowalski. "I'll say something," and he strode to the three steps in front of the stage, took them all in one leap and looked around the room with an expression of pure contempt.

He lifted a fist in an outstretched arm and quickly turned it into a point. He slowly aimed it at everyone in the room in turn, and suddenly roared, "Someone in this room murdered my wife!"

There was another audible gasp as several people looked around.

Ethan moved to Kowalski and put a hand on his shoulder. "Walter—"

"Shut up!" Kowalski roared. He pushed Ethan back against the casket. A couple of the hospital workers got up and eased toward the door.

"Walter!" Ethan shouted.

Kowalski looked at Johnny Lynch in the back of the room and then around at some of the women. "I can only wonder who else she was sleeping around with! And when I find out—"

"Stop!" I heard myself shout. More people got up and scrambled out. All of the hospital people were gone. Lucy and Cindy cringed in their seats. The Funeral Director hastily began wheeling the casket off the stage. I jumped up on the stage myself, quickly followed by Cassius. "Knock it off, Kowalski!"

Ethan was back at him. Before I could reach them, he had a strangle hold around Kowalski's neck. Now Lucy and Cindy got up and ran. Johnny and Ralston were both running to the stage.

Kowalski elbowed backward and caught Ethan in the stomach. He turned just as I got there and whacked Ethan hard across the side of the head, sending him sprawling.

He turned to me and at the same time I gave him a throat jab, and when he grabbed his gagging neck with both hands, I kicked him in the balls as hard as I could. When he bent over, I held his head still as I turned and yelled to Ralston and Johnny.

"Get the women out of here!"

Cassius jumped off the stage as both Ralston and Johnny rushed to Lucy and Cindy, shoving them quickly to the doorway.

I turned back and lifted Kowalski's head by his hair until he was upright. All the nastiness I'd heard had built up in me and I felt myself wanting to deliver a smack for MaryLou. I gave him a devastating right cross to his jaw. He staggered back, bounced off the back edge of the disappearing casket, twisted once and fell off the stage. He lay there, apparently unconscious.

"Come on!" I yelled at Ethan.

He got up and we both leaped off the stage.

Ethan looked back and saw that the Funeral Director had taken charge of MaryLou and was gone. Then he ran to the doorway. Outside we all hustled to Ralston's and Johnny's cars, piled in and screeched away from the church.

Ralston called in a 418 to get help for Kowalski.

We stopped around the corner and put Lucy, Cindy and Cassius in Johnny's car and decided he would take them to Lucy's place, where no one would bother them.

I jumped in Ralston's car and we headed for Johnny's apartment.

Ralston and I would see Walter Kowalski only one more time.

CHAPTER THIRTY-SEVEN

Two mornings later an excited Dr. Feinberg called Bill Ralston.
"I've got some results you're going to like," The M.E. said.

"I could use some," Ralston said. "Shoot."

"But first I've got some totally irrelevant news I'll share with you."

"Irrelevant news is more important than good news?"

The doctor ignored him. "I wanted to call that P.I. guy, Lombardi. But I realize he's a civilian so I thought you should be the one to tell him."

"Doctor, Feinberg, what the hell are you talking about? Tell him what?"

"Mr. Lombardi visited me about a week ago," Feinberg said. "He said he had a hunch, but it was such a long shot he didn't want you to know about it yet."

Ralston perked up. "A hunch? About what?"

"He gave me a pencil belonging to Inspector Lynch. A Giants souvenir pencil, long and thin."

"Goddam it, Doctor! A pencil? What the hell are you talking about?"

"I did some ... er, detective work, you should pardon the expression." He stifled a giggle. Ralston started pacing as he listened. "As you probably know," the M.E. went on, "the lead in a so-called 'lead pencil' isn't lead at all. It's graphite."

"Yeah," Ralston said. "Everybody knows that."

"And graphite is simply powdered carbon. It seems all the graphite used in pencils is imported from either China, Canada,

Mexico or Brazil. And what they do is blend the graphite with clay and a little water, mix it up thoroughly, and then bake it at fifteen hundred degrees to solidify it into varying hardness."

"Uh-huh," Ralston said. "So?"

"So, I figured maybe where the pencil maker gets his graphite, together with the specific formula he uses to harden it, would identify who made the pencil."

"Makes sense, I guess," Ralston said. "Sort of like pizza sauce."

"Exactly," the M.E. said with some glee in his voice. "So, I sent spectrographic samples to all the pencil manufacturers and asked them to identify it, and bingo! The Dixon Ticonderoga company in Florida said it was their graphite in the San Francisco Giants souvenir pencil Mr. Lombardi gave me. None of the other manufacturers claimed it."

"So, what does that tell us?" Ralston asked. "They must make millions of those kinds of pencils."

"Yes, that's the irrelevant part. The really good news is, while I couldn't tell you the pencil he gave me was the murder weapon just because it was a Dixon Ticonderoga, I could tell you beyond a shadow of a doubt that it had microscopic particles of human tissue on its point."

Ralston's eyes lit up. "So that means it *is* the murder weapon?"

"Beyond a shadow of a doubt. Its graphite was the black particles I found on the ear drum in the autopsy."

Ralston was stunned. "Good Lord! Would you testify under oath in court that it's *the* murder weapon? And yes, beyond a shadow of a doubt?"

Slight pause. Then, "Yes, Inspector, I would."

Ralston almost broke his finger calling Steve Lombardi. And when he did, Steve was sick to his stomach.

A grim Bill Ralston, his partner Harvey Keene, and I met at Harrington's saloon at Front and Sacramento that afternoon.

Maybe grim isn't the word for it; we all silently figured we were probably going to a funeral. None of us looked forward to it, but we'd agreed on the phone that it required a head-to-head strategizing session if we were do it correctly and as safely as possible.

Harrington's is a jillion-year-old saloon in the financial district, having been founded and run by a typically Irish family of drinkers and sibling warriors, mostly an aging matriarchal mother, five sons and two sisters. There was another Harrington bar out on Market Street near Van Ness, run by some even more uncles and cousins. I'd known a few of the Harrington brothers and one sister for quite a while, and wouldn't be far off the mark if said that at any given time no two relatives were speaking to each other. It might go toward explaining this to consider that one of the brothers was an ex-seminarian who was kicked out for arguing too much with his teachers and actually punching out one of the priest instructors.

It was usually crowded at lunchtime and Happy Hour, but at 3 p.m. there were a few far corners in which a quiet conversation could be privately held. Other than a few stockbrokers and lawyers remaining at the bar and some late snackers, we had the place to ourselves. Ralston and his partner Keene, being on duty, were in suits for the occasion, Ralston in a light blue necktie and Keene in red-and-maroon regimental stripe. We shook hands without speaking as they sat down. Ralston's jacket was open and I noted his shoulder holster and gold star clipped to his belt.

Finally, after we had our drinks, Ralston looked up.

"Who would have thought," he said. "It's downright depressing, Steve."

I shook my head. "The son of a bitch!" I said, slamming my fist on the table. "The goddamned son of a bitch!"

Ralston and Keene dropped their eyes. No one said anything again for long minutes.

"He always was a hot-head," I said, "but this? He had to be drunk."

"Well, we're here to figure out a plan. I ran a few scenarios past the Captain, and he's on board with whatever I decide. Whatever, though, the SWAT Team is out."

I nodded. "I understand. Arresting a fellow cop at his own residence is far too risky. We know he'll be armed and Johnny's not a guy who'll surrender willingly. Somebody'll get shot before it's over."

Ralston and Keene both nodded. "How about we get him in public somewhere and just close in quickly? Like at dinner somewhere," Keene said.

"Nah," Ralston said. "That would be too quiet an environment. He'd suspect something's up."

"How about we just invite him to meet for a drink? Say, Liverpool Lil's, one of our usual spots. Tell him we have a new lead to discuss," I said.

Ralston perked up. "Better yet, *you* meet him for the drink, at that little table by the window. Have his drink already set up to make sure he's in the seat with his back to the room. Keene and I will be in the men's room and after he sits down, we'll give you five minutes for small talk, then step in and make the arrest. Quick and clean."

"It's gotta be fast," I said. "He'll probably be packing."

"I can cuff him pretty quick," Keene said. "He's never met me and won't recognize me until I've nabbed him. I'll just approach like I'm looking for a seat at the bar."

I shook my head again and took another swig. "I just can't believe it," I said, maybe for the hundredth time in the last five hours. "The guy must have just blown up in a rage."

"I think he'll cop to our scenario," Ralston said.

"He has to," I said. "When Cindy told me that MaryLou intended to tell him she was bisexual, it all fell into focus. They make love, they're laying back, probably looking up at the ceiling, she unloads on him, and in his rage, he grabs the first sharp thing in sight, that souvenir pencil, and jabs her right through the ear."

"Or waits 'til she's asleep, to make it easier," Ralston said.

"And that's when he panics," Keene said.

"Right. Loses all reason. He has to get her out of there, so he wraps her up, drives around town while he tries to think of what to do with her, and in the dead of night decides to throw her off the Lefty O'Doul bridge to make it look like a drowning."

"But she dies on the way," Ralston said. "She's wrapped in a blanket so he doesn't know it."

I shook my head. "Not then. Dr. Feinberg mentioned it to us. Normally, yeah, but he was in a frenzy. Not thinking at all, lost all sense of reason."

"He probably thought she was still alive, just passed out," Keene said.

I shook my head. "Incredible...just fucking incredible!"

Silence again as we all drank. "He couldn't take a chance on her reviving, so he was in a helluva hurry," Ralston added.

"Still, even if he knew she was dead," Keene said. "Drunk, panicked and desperate, he dumps her anyway."

"I'd bet he realized it the second he let go of her," Ralston said.

I shook my head again. "What does it matter?"

More silence. Then, "OK, so when do we do it?" Ralston asked. "I think the sooner the better."

"Tomorrow," I said. "I'll call him in the morning and set it up for three o'clock."

"You got it. I'll clue in the Captain."

The loony Nob Hill parrots were chattering in the trees when I parked outside of Lil's at two forty-five. I was early in order to set up the drinks and make sure Johnny's back was to the rest of the room.

Inside, my heart sank. There were more people than usual at that time of the day.

Damn!

Not only were there three young ladies chatting at the bar directly next to our favorite table, but the damn table was occupied by a professorial type chewing on an unlit pipe and doing a crossword puzzle. He was nursing what looked like a snifter of brandy.

What the hell, I thought as I approached him.

"Pardon me, sir," I smiled. But I'm meeting a guy for an important discussion and this is our favorite table because it's kind of private."

He looked up, surprised. "So?"

"So, would you mind maybe finding another spot and let us have this table?"

"It happens to be my favorite table as well," he said haughtily as he stroked a Fu Manchu beard. "Have your discussion in one of the booths in the back."

"I mean, please, sir? It's too dark in the back to read documents." I looked at my watch.

"Sorry," he said. "I need to read this too." He tapped his puzzle with the stem of his pipe.

I simply didn't have time. I pulled out my PI creds and flashed it at him. "Look, buster," I growled, losing my happy smile. "It's a cop I'm meeting and we're investigating a murder. Now get your ass outta here." I snatched his folded newspaper and handed it back to him. The girls at the bar twirled around in their seats and stared at me.

The guy got up in a hurry and stomped away, muttering. "Sure, sure," he said. "For crissakes."

"Thank you, sir," I called after him. "Order another drink on my tab." He waved a hand in the air without looking back at me.

I motioned to the girls to twirl back and mind their own business. Damn—they were still too close, but I couldn't scoot them away as well, without getting the whole joint gaping at me.

I sat down and checked my watch again. I knew Ralston and Keene were already in the men's room. We only had five minutes to go.

I signaled a waiter over and ordered a scotch for Johnny and a Chardonnay. Nothing suspicious, right?

The drinks came quickly and I put Johnny's at his seat. I looked out the window and saw him cruise by looking for a parking spot, right on time. I took several swigs of my wine and patted my Ruger in its holster. I suddenly couldn't believe this whole thing was happening.

I could feel the sweat forming on my back and my hands were cold. What could go wrong, after all? Well, everything! What if Ralston and Keene were *not* in the men's room? What if they were held up by something? What would I tell Johnny was the reason I had to meet him? What if John smelled a rat when he saw the drinks already set up? What if one of the girls was celebrating a birthday and the place suddenly filled with screaming and giggling women to surprise her? Hell, what if the whole damn University of California Marching Band came in to surprise the owner?

Johnny came in and immediately turned left to our table, nodding at one of the girls. We shook hands and he looked down at his drink.

"In a hurry, are we?"

"Got here early," I shrugged. "I didn't want to get too much of a head start on you." I hoisted my glass and we toasted. "How you doing?"

"Oh, the same," he said. "Bored silly. Can't go anywhere, can't see anybody. Can't hardly leave my apartment."

"We should take in a ball game," I said, suddenly realizing how bad I was at small talk with Johnny. "The Bay Bridge series is coming up with the A's."

"Hell, I hope something shakes down before then," he said. "I've heard they're thinking of a formal indictment."

"Yeah," I said.

Then he said, "So what's up? What have you got?"

Damn, I knew he'd want to get right to the point. I realized that in my anger and stunned despondency I hadn't rehearsed a believable "hot tip" reason to meet him. I took another drink before answering him and signaled the waiter with a "two more" sign.

I pointed to his drink. "Is this an AA meeting?" I grinned. "You on the wagon again?"

He downed the glass without smiling. "Why'd you call? What have you got?" he said again.

"We finally tracked down MaryLou's father," I lied. "Turns out he's in town."

Johnny turned his palms up. "So? You couldn't tell me that on the phone?"

I just looked at him and sipped my drink as if thoughtfully. I figured it *had* to be five minutes by now. I scrabbled for some more small talk.

"What do you think of us trying to track him down? The cops can't find him."

"What, you and me? Are you nuts?" He furrowed his brow at me.

"Is there any chance he knew about you?"

He sat back and banged his glass on the table. "No way," he said defiantly. "She never even spoke to him."

He paused, leaned toward me, and I knew he was sniffing the proverbial rodent.

"Steve, you're beating around the bush. What the fuck's up?"

I took a deep breath. "John, there's been a serious development," I said evenly, noting that he seemed to pick up on my not using the usual "Johnny."

The waiter came with our new round and I used it to stall some more. I made a big deal out of finishing my wine and handing it back to him, along with Johnny's empty glass.

"How serious?" he said. "What's it about?" He looked around, what I thought was nervously. I did too, and saw Keene emerge from the men's room and start to edge his way slowly toward us. I looked at the too-close girls at the bar, getting pumped myself.

"It's all over, Johnny," I said. I made a serious mistake by standing, making it harder for Keene to get to him. "They've got foolproof evidence pointing to you. Cindy blew the whistle about MaryLou coming clean and they figure you lost your temper and stabbed her through the ear into the brain with one of your long Giants pencils. Then you panicked and totally lost it. You thought you'd knocked her out so you drove her to the Lefty O'Doul Bridge and threw her in to make it look like she drowned. Only she was dead already."

His eyes grew wide and he popped up himself. "What? WHAT?" he yelled.

The girls turned again and Keene approached. Johnny instinctively sized him up as a cop. He started to reach inside his jacket to pull out his Smith & Wesson just as Keene got there.

"John, don't!" I yelled. Keene had his cuffs out. "Idiot," I shouted silently. Then I saw that Ralston was right behind him and Johnny recognized him instantly.

"John Lynch, you can come quietly or—"

John fired past Keene right at Ralston, who grabbed his chest and collapsed. The shot rang through the whole place like a bomb going off. The girls screamed.

I darted at John, pulling out my Ruger. Keene whirled and foolishly rushed to Ralston. "Bill! Bill!"

Just as I was about to reach Johnny, he took two fast jumps to the bar and grabbed one of the girls. All three of them were still screaming. The entire saloon seemed to be yelling.

Johnny took the girl by the neck as a shield and turned to me, pointing his gun.

"Don't do it, Johnny! Give it up!"

"Stay away, Stevie! I've got nothing to lose now." He backed slowly toward the door. The girl kept screaming, her eyes wide with fear and her hands groping at Johnny's arm around her neck.

I saw Keene on his police radio shouting for backup and an ambulance. "This is Inspector Keene at Liverpool Lil's! We have a 406 Officer down," he was yelling. *"406 Officer down!"*

I stepped slowly toward Johnny, but letting him get some distance as he backed toward the door.

"Let her go, Johnny!"

"I swear I'll blast her, Stevie. Let me get to my car."

He kept the gun pressed tightly to the girl's temple.

"Drop her now, John. Don't do this."

He started stepping quickly, still backing up and dragging the girl with him along the sidewalk. I put my finger through the trigger guard and held up my dangling gun in the air and put my own hands up. I could hear distant sirens.

I heard Keene knock over an outside patio chair and fire his gun at Johnny from behind me. He missed and John fired back, also missing.

As he did so the girl reached back and jabbed her fingers into one of his eyes. She screamed again as John let go of her. She dropped to the ground and rolled into the gutter.

John uttered a loud growl as he reached up to his face.

I was in a dream. I had no idea what was going on and I carefully dropped to one knee, spotted my Ruger's laser on Johnny's chest and shot the best friend I ever had.

He dropped his gun and lurched backward as if yanked by an unseen cable, falling on his back to the ground. I rushed up to him and knelt just as two patrol cars and an ambulance pulled up.

"Lieutenant Ralston's hit!" I yelled at them. "Inside!"

It seemed like the whole world was exploding.

He looked up at me with staring eyes.

"Johnny, you stupid son of a bitch! What the hell—? "

His face was blurred through my tears as in my mind I was shaking a movie star-handsome young Inspector's hand as his new partner. I saw him writing anonymous checks he couldn't afford to widows and over-tipping waiters in Hunter's Point bars and weeping openly at funerals.

"Stevie," he whispered, gripping my other arm. "I really fucked up ... didn't I?"

I cradled his head in my arms and buried my dripping eyes in his hair.

"Yes, you did, you stupid, dumb, Irish bastard."

"Royally, huh?" he gasped.

"Royally," I said.

And he closed his eyes as his last breath rushed past my ear.

EPILOGUE

It's a weird feeling to attend the funeral of the man you killed.

Weirder still to be one of only four people present besides the dead guy: his lover's husband; the man the dead guy shot; a priest, and me. Seems like the setup for a bad joke, but now was not the time.

Since John Timothy Lynch had no living relatives, I assumed responsibility for giving him at least a semblance of a Catholic funeral and burial. But then harsh reality hit me and I realized my pittance of a bank account wouldn't buy one handle on a casket. When I had Ralston check John's bank account, I found he had a pretty good stash, but we couldn't touch a penny of it. I discovered that in cases of someone having no living relatives it fell into the jurisdiction of the San Francisco Public Administrator, whose responsibility it then became to find any relative anywhere who would get whatever bank account Johnny had. I'm not a lawyer, but it was that word "anywhere" that bugged me. I quickly imagined a heretofore unknown second- or third-besotted cousin in some god-forsaken hick village in Ireland jumping on the next Aer Lingus jet to SFO to collect his surprise fortune!

When I explained this to Ralston he came through like a trooper. He volunteered to front the money we needed and I could repay him half when I hit my next big job. I showed my good faith by giving him a promissory note for a blank amount, and we were off to the races.

I bought Johnny a bargain-priced casket, rented a viewing room at a local funeral parlor, and found a retired old Irish priest at

St. Anne's with an honest-to-goodness brogue to say a few words—which I had written for him.

The viewing area was a silent room with only a gently hushed organ piped in, playing "Danny Boy," which I guessed was the only Irish song the Funeral Director could find. In little recessed shelves around the room were statues of Catholic saints—half of them men and half women. Velvet draperies hung along the walls and directly behind the casket was a magnificent Crucifix. I even had the casket open, as almost every living Irishman would want.

Ralston had made a commendable recovery for just four days. The slug had skidded off his Kevlar vest and into his arm, which was now in a sling and strapped to his waist. He still could not sit down and stand up without worrying his twisting torso would jerk the sling and rip open the stitches, so he stood in the back leaning on the wall. We gave each other a solemn head nod, as one does at funerals.

We were pretty spread out, which made the whole scene even weirder. I sat in the first row of uncomfortable wooden folding chairs in an end seat, Walter Kowalski seven rows back, in a seat on the other end, and Ralston.

When Walter had slinked in through the back curtain I had almost fainted in surprise. Now he approached me as we waited for the priest.

"What are you doing here?" I asked him.

"I had to see the guy," he growled back. "The guy who killed my wife."

"Well be quick about it. This isn't doing anyone any good."

"I heard you were the one to do it," he said to me.

"Yeah, wasn't how it was supposed to happen."

He countered, "None of this was supposed to happen."

He had a point. "OK, you've seen him. Now get the hell out of here."

He retreated and I took another seat near the casket. Soon I heard the curtain rustle in the back of the room and a distant front door slam as Walter marched out.

The priest began the service by forgetting what I had written and reading from a small book with black leather covers. Funny how many sermons are the same regardless of the life the man led. We were at the funeral of a murderer, yet the priest was saying the same words he may recite over the funeral for a beloved grandmother of twelve. But he finally came to the words I had provided him.

And my tears finally came. I put my face in my hands as the priest finished and blessed the corpse, and I suddenly felt Ralston's palm on my shoulder, squeezing it gently and saying nothing.

Johnny ... Johnny ...!

Neither Ralston nor I wanted to say anything aloud, so we just rose as the priest left. I shamelessly dried my eyes with my handkerchief as we walked out into an overcast chill and got in my car. We drove to the cemetery, following a single hearse and the priest in his own car. After a few more words about death and the hereafter, it was over.

I turned in the damp mist of Colma and looked left toward the invisible city. Ralston was halfway through a drag of his cigarette.

He coughed as we headed toward the car. "Should you really be doing that in your condition?" I asked.

"What condition is that?" He smiled and looked at his cigarette. "This isn't the most dangerous object to try and kill me this week."

"That's true."

We stopped and stood in silence next to each other. I had been thinking of a quote from a South American writer I always admired, Jorge Luis Borges. It went, "The future is inevitable and precise, but it may not occur. God lurks in the gaps." I don't know why it applied to this moment, but it does.

I turned back to the car when Ralston grabbed me by the arm. "Steve," he said.

"Yeah."

"I want to tell you what I would have said in the funeral parlor."

"Shoot," I replied, unaware of the poor choice of words.

"It's something he always said to me when I was a rookie. 'Just worry about making today happy. If you string enough of those happy todays together, you'll have a happy life.'"

213

"A happy life," I pondered. "Guess we need to start over again today and see how long we can make it."

I walked away, toward the car.

Ralston shuffled and caught up with me. "Buy you a drink?"

"Sure. Where to?"

"Where else?" he said.

We got in the car and headed back to town. On the way, I said, "So, you guys never found out who tipped off Hiram in the first place?"

He shook his head. "Nope. Phone records showed nothing, so we figured it must have been an email. But he didn't have a computer. So, we had the rangers search his place for a letter, but zip. Never did figure it out."

"And you didn't find old Hiram himself, either?"

"Nothing," he said. "He never turned up in Mooringsport, as far as we know. Either he's pretty damn clever or he jumped off the bridge."

I laughed. "I guess if he ever does turn up back there and visit his wife's grave, when he sees MaryLou ... well, we'll hear from him eventually. Maybe through Ethan."

We turned off the freeway and down Van Ness, turned on Greenwich and headed for Lil's. We heard sirens behind us, and I pulled over. Two fire engines screamed past, followed closely by an ambulance.

We pulled back in traffic and turned on Lyon. Down the street toward Lil's the fire trucks had stopped and plumes of ugly black smoke rose from the right side of the street.

We parked, walked over to the left sidewalk and down toward Lil's.

When we got there, we were stunned.

Across the street, Liverpool Lil's was burning to the ground.

The End